The Daughters of America Emergency Service !

When two lovely young members of this U.S. welfare organization were killed in South America, it seemed only a tragic accident. But then the New York D.A.M.E.S. office revealed that the girls in the wreck were impostors, not members of D.A.M.E.S. at all—and the F.B.I. confirmed that both girls had long criminal records.

What had they been doing in Brazil in this strange masquerade?

Illya and Napoleon investigated . . . and found a secret construction project deep in the wilderness, where THRUSH was building a startling new weapon for world conquest. They had to be stopped—but the project was protected in an impregnable fortress under tons and tons of water!

This is the ninth in Ace Books' series of exciting MAN FROM U.N.C.L.E. novels. For information on earlier books, see page 160.

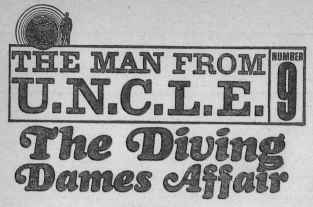

THE MAN FROM U.N.C.L.E.
NUMBER 9

The Diving Dames Affair

by Peter Leslie.

ACE BOOKS, INC.
1120 Avenue of the Americas
New York, N.Y. 10036

THE DIVING DAMES AFFAIR

Copyright ©, 1967, by Metro-Goldwyn-Mayer, Inc.

All Rights Reserved

THE DIVING DAMES AFFAIR

THERE WERE TWO BLONDES in the red convertible. White teeth gleamed in tanned faces as the car swept past Miguel Oliveira on his mule and then braked for the first of the hairpin bends leading down the mountainside to the main road and to Rio de Janeiro. The old man turned and watched it out of sight around a corner of the sun-baked rock face. Plenty of young people drove up here in the weekends, but it was unusual to see two girls in a car alone. He listened to the squealing of tires and the rising bellow of the exhaust as the convertible accelerated away from the turn, then transferred his gaze to the brush-covered rocky precipice dropping away to his right. Presently the car reappeared on a loop of road far below him, chrome glinting in the bright light as it arrowed down towards the last of the bends.

Sixty feet below the parapet guarding the curve, the broad highway to the state capital bisected the valley. And just beyond the corner, hidden from the girls in the low sports car but clearly visible to Miguel Oliveira, the driver of a decrepit truck who had found he was on the wrong road was laboriously turning.

The convertible entered the hairpin too fast. Oliveira saw its brake lights blaze as the blonde driver stamped on the pedal. The car slewed sideways, was expertly corrected, and snaked out of the bend to find the road-

5

way almost completely blocked by the truck. Again the twin lights glowed—and then the girl, realizing that she could never stop in time, swung the wheel over in a desperate attempt to squeeze through between the radiator of the truck and the parapet. But the car, already partially out of her control, lurched sideways again and slammed into the low wall.

As Oliviera watched, horrified, it burst through the parapet, rose into the air, and hung for an instant motionless before plunging out of sight onto the steep slope linking the side road with the highway below. While the truck driver was erupting from his cabin to run to the edge, a cloud of dust mushroomed up over the shattered wall.

Seconds later, it seemed to the old man, the sound of the impact floated up the mountainside.

"Will they live?" the police captain asked the hospital intern later.

The young doctor raised white-coated shoulders in a professional shrug. "Barring unforeseen complications," he said. "It was fortunate for them that it was an open car. They were both thrown out before it landed upside down on the rock."

"And their injuries?"

"Multiple contusions and extensive lacerations in each case. The girl who was driving broke both legs against the steering wheel as she came out, but the other one's really worse off: there were boulders where she landed, and she has a cracked skull, a fractured pelvis and several broken ribs."

"They're still unconscious, both of them?"

The intern nodded. "And likely to remain so for some time. It was nearly half an hour before the ambulance got to them—and the sun's fierce at that time in the afternoon."

The policeman sighed. "I suppose we'd better go through the motions, then," he said, flicking a speck of dust from his olive green jacket. "I'll have to make a report, get in touch with next of kin, and so on. Shall we have a look at their effects?"

The doctor nodded again and led the way to an anteroom at the far end of the rubber tiled hospital corridor. A highway patrolman sprang to attention and saluted as the two men entered. Behind him, the sounds of suburban traffic filtered through green shutters closing out the dusk.

"Ah, Gomez," the police captain said, returning the salute. "What have we found out about these unfortunate ladies?"

The man looked uncomfortable. "Captain," he said, "I am very sorry, but . . . there is nothing."

"Nothing? But their names, surely? Their addresses?"

Gomez shook his head slowly. "Nothing," he repeated. "No driving license, no insurance certificate, no passports, no papers at all. I think they are Americans, but so far I have been unable to find out anything about their identity."

The captain stared in disbelief. "That is very curious," he said at last. "Let us see if perhaps their clothes . . ."

He moved across the room to a table on which were laid out two handbags and their contents, a pair of shattered sunglasses, shoes, several tourist's road maps, an entertainment guide to Rio, and two piles of bloodstained clothing.

"I'm afraid we had to cut the clothes quite a bit," to get them off . . ." the doctor began apologetically.

"It does not matter," the policeman said. He picked up the ripped garments gingerly, one by one, and examined them: brightly colored blouses, underclothes, a skirt, a garter belt, what had once been a pair of white slacks. Finally he dropped the last one back on the table and turned to the doctor.

"The man is right," he said. "This is very odd: not one of these things has a name tag on it. Moreover, the labels and makers' names have been removed also."

"It is the same with the handbags, Captain," the patrolman interrupted. "See—cigarettes, lighters, money, lipsticks and compacts, keys, suntan oil, tissues . . . but no letters, no papers of any kind."

"Evidently," the captain said, "these are ladies who wished to remain incognito. But we have our duty to

7

perform. We must find out who they are so that their relatives can be informed. We must force ourselves to be ungallant enough to unmask them."

Gomez smiled dutifully. "Yes, Captain," he murmured.

"No doubt the laboratory could eventually trace them through these clothes and the shoes, but for an ordinary road accident it hardly seems . . ." The captain paused. "What about the accident, by the way?" he inquired. "How did it happen? What do the witnesses say?"

"There were witnesses in three different cars on the highway. But all they saw was the second part of the accident, as it were. They saw the car bounce down the bank after it had broken through the parapet of the road above."

"Were there no witnesses up there?"

"We have found none."

"But what caused the accident? Why did the car break through the parapet?"

"We could find no reason for that either. There are two skid marks just *after* the hairpin, about a hundred and fifty yards before the place where the wall is breached—as though someone had braked hard there. But of course they could have been made by some other car."

"Quite," the captain said dryly. "So there are no marks at all—other than the broken wall—where the car left the road?"

"No, sir. None at all."

"This begins to get very puzzling. What about the car itself?"

"It was an Alfa Romeo 2600—a beautiful car," Gomez said, his face lighting up with the enthusiasm of the car aficionado. "It is completely wrecked. Beyond any hope of repair."

"Yes, Gomez, yes," the captain prompted gently. "No doubt. But what I meant was—what is its number, where does it come from, and was there anything interesting in it?"

"Oh, I see. I'm sorry, sir. . . . No, there was nothing at all in it of interest. A Japanese transistor radio and a pair

8

of string gloves in the cubbyhole; a flask of brandy that was smashed in a door pocket. No papers."

"And the owner's name?"

"It was a rented car, Captain. Locally registered and belonging to a garage two blocks inland from Copacabana."

"Ah. No doubt the rental company can give us a lead on the person who rented it, then."

"Yes, sir. Da Silva's over there now making inquiries."

But the rental company was unable to reveal the names either of the driver or her companion. The car had been rented on behalf of an organization.

"D-A-M-E-S?" the police captain spelled out slowly in his office the next morning. "What on earth does that stand for?"

"It's a *yanqui* welfare organization," the patrolman called Da Silva said. "It means . . ." He consulted a piece of paper in his hand. "It means Daughters of America Missionary Emergency Service."

"Missionaries! They don't look like missionaries! And what are they doing here? I've never heard of them. Do they have an office here—if indeed these women belong to the organization?"

"From the descriptions, they're the ones who booked the car, all right. They're not exactly missionaries as such—the D.A.M.E.S. is one of those charitable trusts that does good work wherever it's needed. Looking after earthquake survivors, helping famine victims, and so on."

"But we don't have any earthquakes or famine in Rio!"

"No, sir. We don't have a D.A.M.E.S. office either."

"Perhaps it's just as well. . . . Did anyone think to check the mileage on the car speedometer with the mileage logged by the garage when it was hired?"

Da Silva's plump cheeks widened in a self-congratulatory smile. "Yes, Captain. I got the figures from the garage and went over to look at the car early this morning. It had covered nearly fifteen hundred miles since it was rented three days ago."

"Good. If they didn't have passports with them, they couldn't have crossed the frontier, so let's see. . . ."

9

The captain rose from his desk, took off his jacket and draped it over the back of his chair, picked up a pair of dividers and walked to a large wall map. The ceiling fan in that corner of the room stirred the hot, heavy air and detached a tendril of hair from his carefully groomed head as he applied the dividers to the scale.

"Yes," he said a moment later. "As I thought . . . they could have been to Porto Alegre, Bahia or Brasilia—or for that matter they could have done lots of little trips locally. But get in touch with our people in those places and ask if *they* have any mission or bureau run by the D-A-whatever-it-is."

"Yes, sir."

The officer sat down at his desk again. He took a small hand mirror from a drawer and studied his face. Above the thin moustache, there were hollows in his cheeks and the sallow skin below his eyes was pouched and puffy. He was already overworked: there had been a series of burglaries with violence in his subdivision and his superiors were pressing for results. Now he was burdened with this extra mystery. If only, he thought, the *yanqui* girls had written off their car further away from the city, or waited until the weather was less oppressive. . . .

He loosened his tie and patted his forehead with a white handkerchief. "I'm not happy with this business of the witnesses," he said, combing his hair into place and putting the mirror back in its drawer. "Surely somebody must have seen what happened; something must have made that car break through the wall! Put out a radio message—you know: an accident occurred . . . a red sports car left the road . . . two foreign women were gravely injured . . . will anyone who witnessed the affair please contact us. The old routine."

"Very well, Captain."

"And Da Silva—you'd better take Gomez and go back to the hospital. If these girls are still unconscious, take their fingerprints and wire them to New York. In the matter of identification, we can probably save ourselves a lot of trouble that way."

CONTENTS

Chapter 1

Briefing For Solo

THERE WERE FOUR pieces of paper on the huge desk presided over by Alexander Waverly, head of the Policy and Operations Department of the organization designated by the letters U.N.C.L.E.—the United Network Command for Law and Enforcement.

The Command's headquarters faced the slender monolith of the United Nations building in New York (although in fact only a single window, the one in Waverly's office, linked the building with the open air, the rest being sheathed by a row of seedy brownstone buildings, a public garage, and a restaurant-"key" club). From it, a network of communications and agents of all nationalities fanned out over the world to combat threats to peace and good order wherever and whatever they might be. The problem occupying Alexander Waverly at this moment was whether the four pieces of paper on his desk added up to such a threat.

His lean, lined face crumpled into a grimace of exasperation as he took a briar pipe from the pocket of his baggy tweed suit and shuffled the papers around with the stem. Two of them were carbon flimsies, one was a short newspaper cutting pasted onto a sheet of typing paper, and the last was a leaf torn from a desk memorandum on which a single word was scrawled in pencil. He shook his gray head, pursed his lips, and finally pressed one of a row of buttons set into a platen on the desk.

"Yes, Mr. Waverly?" The girl's voice came from a concealed speaker somewhere behind the paneling.

"Ask Mr. Solo to come in, please," Waverly said into the air—and he slumped into the chair behind the desk and began filling his pipe from a Dresden jar. There were already two other pipes—a Meerschaum and a cherrywood—filled but unsmoked on the desk.

In a few minutes Napoleon Solo knocked and came in—medium height, compact figure, brown eyes below crisp, dark hair, and a determined chin which offset a mouth frequently curved in an ironic smile.

"I'd like you to have a look at these, Mr. Solo," Waverly said, laying down the briar and flicking three of the pieces of paper across the polished wood of his desk.

Solo sat down and picked up the sheets. The cutting was from that morning's edition of one of the New York papers. It was clipped from an inside page below the fold, and was headed DAMES IN DISTRESS. The story read:

Rio de Janeiro, Wednesday.—Two young women, believed to be American citizens, were seriously injured in an automobile accident near the Brazilian ex-capital last night when their sports car crashed through the retaining wall of a mountain road and fell to the highway below. They are thought to be members of a Daughters of America Missionary Emergency Service (D.A.M.E.S.) team. Every effort is being made to establish the identity of the two women, both of whom were still unconscious early today.

One of the carbons was a copy of a letter from the D.A.M.E.S. headquarters in the East Fifties to Police Headquarters in Rio. It was signed "Barbara Stretford" and stated succinctly that the Service had no teams at present operating in Rio, Porto Alegre, Brasilia, or indeed any place in Brazil. The other was a copy of a cable to the same address from the FBI. It read:

270767/0815 YOUR 260767/1435 STOP PRINTS IDENTIFY AAA RITA ROSENTHAL TWENTY-SIX CONVICTED LOS ANGELES 1963 FELONY 1965 1966 FRAUD BBB BERNADINE SCIOTTO TWENTYTHREE CONVICTED BERKELEY 1964 FELONY PRESENTLY WANTED FRAUD CHARGES IOWA STOP AIRMAILED DETAILS FOLLOW PLEASE DETAIN BBB AND ADVISE.

Napoleon Solo placed the papers carefully back on

the desk and raised quizzical eyebrows at his chief. "And the fourth?" he asked.

Waverly spun around the memo sheet so that he could read it. The penciled scrawl read: *Solo?*

"I'm afraid I don't quite understand," Solo said. "So two girls falsely representing themselves as members of D.A.M.E.S. almost write themselves off in Brazil. What does that have to do with us—or with me?"

"The balance of probabilities have to do with us, Mr. Solo," Waverly said. "You state the problem too simply. The newspaper cutting was one of the minor pieces of trivia that come my way. I should doubtless never have given it a second thought, had I not run into Mrs. Stretford this morning. She happened to mention this odd query from the Rio police. And then, as a matter of routine, I found the FBI cable among the sheaf of courtesy copies they provide me with every day."

"Yes, but—"

"Patience, Mr. Solo. Patience! I was still disposed to file the matter away in my mind as an oddity—but then Forster of the Central Intelligence Agency telephoned me to ask what I thought of it."

"The C.I.A.! And what *do* you think of it?"

"I really don't know," Waverly said frankly. "Here we have two American citizens, both with police records, passing themselves off in a friendly foreign country as members of an eminently respectable trust based in New York. It's curious, to say the least. One wonders exactly why."

"Your papers don't say much about the D.A.M.E.S. angle."

"No, but I have been in touch with Rio by radio. Their car was hired and all the documents they produced were on official D.A.M.E.S. paper. Yet *in* the car they appear to have gone to a great deal of trouble to remove any reference to the organization—or to their identity at all. There were no papers, no licenses, no insurance certificates, no letters among their effects. And even their clothes had all the tabs removed."

"That *is* strange," Solo admitted. "You'd think that anyone who bothered to sail under the wrong flag, as it

15

were, would keep it flying especially bravely, to foster the illusion."

"Exactly. There may be nothing more to it, of course, than a simple case of intended fraud or false pretenses. Some kind of confidence trick. On the other hand . . ."

"Any particular reason for the C.I.A. interest?"

"No, just routine. The facts I've given you are enough to make them wonder. But they're not sufficiently interested to risk their necks. You know how delicately they have to move these days: everything they do is wrong, everywhere. They're the whole world's whipping boy. And with the congress of Pan-American states and the O.A.S. conference coming up, Forster's especially keen to avoid treading on Brazilian toes. If they should go blundering in there and there's nothing to this thing, you can imagine what the Latin American papers would make of it!"

Solo nodded. "And they want us to be the fall guys, is that it?"

"As we're an international organization, it would look much better if there *were* any trouble. Since you're not engaged on anything specific at the moment," Waverly said almost apologetically, "I thought you might like to run down to Rio and, ah, nose around for a day or so."

"What exactly do you want me to do?"

"Be discreet above all. Try to find out what these girls were doing and why; find out where they are based and if there are any more of them. And don't declare yourself: you're strictly on your own. As I say, there's probably nothing in it, but I daresay it's worth a couple of days of your time."

"I can't go officially to the Rio police?"

"No."

"Well, the first thing, obviously, is to see the injured parties. Any objection if I present myself to the hospital —and to the police if necessary—as an American lawyer acting for them?"

"I don't think so. Just so long as nobody is involved officially before you find out what's going on. If in fact it turns out to be merely a police matter, you can simply report back to me and we'll hand the facts over to the proper authorities. If, on the other hand, this affair *is* the tip of some—ah—international iceberg of wrong-doing, then we shall probably have to state our case and ask for Brazilian cooperation."

Solo rose to his feet. "All right, then," he said. "I'll be on my way. If I hurry, I should be able to make the afternoon plane.

Waverly nodded. "I'll have Miss Tanimotu telephone for your ticket now," he said. "You can pick up a few notes I've made from Operations, and I'll send Geddes to meet you at the airport with a suitable passport, papers, cover story and so on."

"I'll be in touch by radio," Solo said. And he walked briskly out.

During the lunch hour, one of the switchboard girls from the vast U.N.C.L.E. communications center on the second floor of the headquarters went to a drugstore. After she had eaten, she went to the telephone booth in the back and dialed a number. She spoke rapidly and concisely for half a minute and then returned to her seat for coffee.

The fat man to whom she had been speaking replaced the receiver on its cradle in the Park Avenue penthouse. He sat for a few moments drumming ringed fingers on a Sheraton occasional table. Then he reached for the instrument again.

"Hello, operator?" he said. "Will you give me Long Distance, International? I want to make a call to Rio de Janeiro."

Chapter 2

The Man On The Mule

PALM TREES LINED the private road leading to the hospital and punctuated the green verandas surrounding the low, white building. From the steps leading to the entrance, a bright crescent of sand and surf marking the distant waterfront was visible between two soaring apartment buildings further down the hill. Away to the right, above a colony of flat-roofed villas, the Sugarloaf humped itself into the sky at the seaward end of the chain of tree-covered mountains encircling the city.

Napoleon Solo braked the hired Buick to a halt on the graveled circle and ran up the steps to the foyer. His oatmeal-colored lightweight suit clung uncomfortably to shoulders and thighs. After the long flight and a sleepless night in a hotel room, he was exhausted by the unaccustomed heat.

A large pendant fan revolved slowly in the shadowy entrance hall. Beneath it, a uniformed police officer was speaking to the dark girl at the reception desk. Under her starched cap, the girl flashed a professionally inquiring smile at Solo. The agent placed his brief case on the desk and leaned forwards. "My name is Williams," he said. "I'm a New York attorney delegated to represent two patients you have here: Miss Rosenthal and Miss Sciotto—the two Americans injured in the auto crash. Have they regained consciousness, do you know; and, if so, may I see them?"

The police officer had swung around and was staring curiously at Solo. His sallow, moustached face was tired. As the receptionist was about to speak he interrupted. "Captain Garcia at your service, Mr. Williams," he said, holding out his hand. "Evidently you have not heard."

"Heard?" Solo repeated, taking the hand. "Heard what, Captain?"

"Both the ladies are dead, senhor," the girl said.

"Dead?" Solo echoed. "Both of them? But I thought—"

"They were both improving, though it is true that neither had recovered consciousness. But then something . . . happened." The girl glanced at Garcia.

"Regrettably—most regrettably—there seems to have been somebody with an interest in seeing that they never did recover consciousness," the policeman supplied.

"Do you mean that they were killed? Murdered?"

"Unfortunately. We might very well have accepted that they had succumbed to their injuries, were it not for the fact that the intruder left open a window that should have been closed. But once we were suspicious, we were able to ask the post-mortem doctor to—how do you say?—keep the open eye. He found that, beyond all doubt, they had been killed by that simplest of all methods: the air bubble injected straight into a vein by a hypodermic syringe. . . ."

"I have no wish to be obtrusive, Captain," Solo said later in Garcia's office, "and as a lawyer, of course, I have no right at all to question you—but as a matter of interest, do you have any idea why these girls were killed, or who killed them?"

"None, Mr. Williams. At the same time—purely as a matter of interest, of course—I am curious to know how these ladies managed to instruct an attorney to come all the way from New York to represent them, when in fact they had never recovered consciousness after the accident. An accident they presumably never knew had occurred."

Solo smiled. "I confess my Portuguese at fault in expressing myself poorly," he lied easily. "I said delegated to represent them. I am not of course instructed by the victims. That would, as you say, have been impossible. I was asked to come by the organization to which they falsely claimed to belong, the D.A.M.E.S. The directors naturally wish to know why they are being thus misrepresented. I had hoped to find out for them by questioning the ladies."

"Ah. You were to hold what is called, I believe, a watching brief?"

"Exactly. Any information you are permitted to give me will therefore be of the greatest assistance."

"There is very little," Garcia said wearily. "The car was rented on behalf of the organization and they gave, at the time, no names. It was paid for in advance and the papers and indemnities they produced seemed to be in order."

"Was the accident itself . . . engineered?"

"We think not. At the time there were no direct witnesses—only passersby on the lower road who saw the car tumble down the slope. But after putting out a radio message, we pulled in a truck driver who seems to have been the unwitting cause of the affair. He had taken the wrong road and was making an illegal turn just before a sharp bend. The sports car hit the wall and went over in attempting to avoid him."

"He did not come forward at the time?"

"No. He drove away because he was frightened he would be blamed."

"I see. Then it looks very much as though . . . You have not found out where the women were based? Where they came from?"

"Not yet, senhor. It is a big country with many states. We shall find out."

"Of course. It looks, then, as though they may have been killed to delay that investigation?"

"Yes," Garcia said with a sigh. "I suppose it does."

Solo found the site of the accident without any trouble. He had not liked to ask the policeman any further details: as a lawyer, he could have no possible interest in viewing the place. But from local newspaper reports, he was able to identify the highway—and once there, the evidence was all too plain. The brushwood was still scarred and flattened where the breakdown cranes had penetrated to haul away the wrecked car. Above, a trail of stones fanned out from the breached wall of the side road curving up around the flank of the mountain.

The agent took the minor road and left his car a hundred yards below the hairpin. There was nothing to see, really—just the broken parapet and the remains of chalk marks made by the police investigators on the scorching macadam. Nearer the corner, where the foliage on the mountainside shimmered in the heat haze rising from the road, four black skid marks angled across the surface. The car had obviously been out of alignment, going partially sideways, when the driver braked. *She must have taken the bend too fast, seen the truck, clamped on the anchors when she had already lost the back end, and then released them and tried to get through,* Solo thought to himself.

He walked around the curve and crouched down to the height the driver of a sports car would have been.

20

As he had thought, the road beyond the hairpin was invisible.

There was not much traffic. An ancient bus full of Negro women in bright headscarves rattled down towards the main road in low gear; a tan Chevrolet hissed past on its way up into the mountains. He walked slowly back to his car, fanning his face with a newspaper. By the Buick, an old man with a wide-brimmed straw hat and a blanket over one shoulder had halted his mule. Solo gave him good-day politely.

"Good day, senhor," the old man replied. "And a good route to you. It is a good day for those who travel prudently. But no day is good for those who would arrive before their time . . . the *yanqui* ladies whose haste brought them only to the disaster you have been investigating, for example."

"You saw the accident?"

"Naturally. I am always on this road at this time."

"But . . . you did not come forward in answer to the police radio message?"

"The senhor will forgive me—but he is perhaps of the police himself?"

"No, no. My name is Williams; I am an attorney. I am trying to find out what caused the accident. I represent the ladies."

"So. A lawyer. Miguel Oliveira at your service," the old man said courteously, holding out a seamed hand. "As to the matter of the police, when you reach my age you learn that is wisest to avoid any unnecessary contact with them. I have seen many different police forces —and today's friend may be tomorrow's enemy. Also I do not possess a radio."

"But you did see the accident," Solo said, shaking the hand. "Can you advance any . . . Why do you think it happened?"

"They were going too fast. There was a truck. But then they always went too fast. Man is not intended for such speeds."

"Always? You had seen the girls before?"

"Many times, senhor. In different cars. Perhaps three

times each month, perhaps five. They could not have been here more often for they lived so far away."

"You know where they came from?" Solo asked in astonishment.

"Si, senhor. From far, from very far away, as I have said."

"Do you know what place, what town?"

"That I cannot tell you. But it was very far. Many hundreds, perhaps thousands of miles. Beyond the mountains, across the plain, beyond the great forests, beyond Belo Horizonte, beyond Goiania, somewhere in the hills of the interior before the great new city that men say rises like white towers into the sky."

"You mean Brasilia?"

"I believe that is what it is called," Miguel Oliveira admitted graciously.

"But . . . but . . . how in the world—you will forgive me, senhor? —how can you know this?"

"Simply," the old man said. He extended an arm up towards the tree-covered crests piercing the aching blue of the sky. On the road somewhere above, an automobile windshield flashed fiercely in the sun. "Below the pass, Pedro Gonzales keeps a small shack where he sells trinkets and refreshing drinks to the tourists who stop to admire the view. Each day, I pause to bid him good-day and to drink a little wine with him. On two occasions, I have heard the American women make a telephone call from there. They also drink there—and I understand some American, although I do not speak it very well."

"You heard what they said? You heard the exchange they called?"

"I cannot recall the name. But on each occasion, it seemed to be a name unknown to the operator. The lady telephoning insisted, and said, yes, it was the correct name—it was a place in the mountains before that city, where they make a new lake."

"A small place in the mountains behind Brasilia where they're building an artificial lake—probably a dam," Solo said. "Senhor Oliveira, you have been more than helpful. I cannot thank you enough."

"It is nothing, senhor."

"One more question I must ask you. If you could see both the car and the truck, you must have been some way further up the hill. Did you see anything else—anything at all—which might have had anything to do with the accident? Was there anyone else around, near the scene of the disaster?"

"No, there was nothing. Just the car and the truck. If there had been anything, I would have seen it."

"Thank you again," Solo said—and he ran back to the Buick, turned, and headed for the main road and Rio.

"God go with you," the old man replied, urging his mule to resume its laborious climb.

The driver of the tan Chevrolet, who had been following Napoleon Solo ever since he had left the airport, put away his binoculars and opened the trunk of the car. He propped open the lid of a small short-wave transceiver and fiddled with switches and dials. Then he held a single can to one ear and spoke softly into a hand microphone.

"Greerson," he said. "The subject visited the hospital this morning and left with Garcia, the police captain. He stayed some time in Garcia's office, called on the rental company, a couple of newspaper offices, and then drove out to the place where the girls left the road. . . . He's just spent a quarter of an hour searching the area and yacking to some peasant on a mule. Then he turned and headed back for the city. . . . Okay, Schwarz had better pick him up at the next intersection: he saw me pass while he was on the road. . . . What's that? . . . Oh, him. Sure I will. Right away. . . ."

He swung the Chevrolet around and went slowly back down the hill. After the third hairpin, he saw Miguel Oliveira jogging slowly towards him on the mule.

The man called Greerson drove a few yards past and braked. He got out of the car and called after the old man: "Hey! You!"

The mule continued its upward plod. The old man did not turn his head. Swearing, the driver of the Chevrolet dropped his cigarette to the ground, swiveled his heel on the butt, and shouted again: "Hey, old man! Are you deaf?"

This time, Oliveira turned his head. He spoke without checking the pace of the mule. "Are you addressing me, senhor?"

"Of course I'm addressing you, you old fool," Greerson snapped in his bad Portuguese. "Do you see anyone else around?"

The old man halted the beast and sat waiting patiently while Greerson strode up to him. "What do you want with me, senhor?" he said.

"First, I want to teach you to speak when you're spoken to, peasant. Get off that mule."

Oliveira sat silent and regarded him impassively.

"I said get off!" Greerson shouted. He raised his right forearm across his chest and struck the old man viciously, backhanded, on the face. Oliveira's broad-brimmed hat fell to the ground. His leathery cheek had flushed a dull red with the blow. And still he stared unwinkingly at his attacker.

Greerson hit him again: a wicked right to the solar plexus. The old man gave a choking grunt, folded forwards over the neck of the mule, and slid to the ground.

The driver of the Chevrolet drew back a foot with a pointed shoe and kicked him, once on the side of the head and twice in the kidneys. After a while, Oliveira rolled slowly over and tried to sit up, supporting himself on gnarled hands. "Why . . . why do you do this to me, senhor?" he croaked. A thin thread of scarlet ran from one side of his bruised mouth.

Measuring his distance carefully, Greerson drew back his foot for the fourth time. He caught the old man full on the chin with the iron-studded heel. This time, he did not get up.

The rasping of a cicada in a tree across the road shivered the hot silence as Greerson, panting, straightened his tie, smoothed down the front of his jacket, and looked cautiously around. The stretch of road between the hairpins lay empty in the sun. Neither human beings nor vehicles broke the succession of wooded undulations

24

rising to the brassy sky. The mule stood motionless in a patch of shadow cast by a stunted oak, its head hanging low.

Bending down, Greerson seized the unconscious figure of Miguel Oliveira by the shoulders, hauling it into the roadway not too far from the spots of blood that were already darkly congealing in the dust of the roadside.

After a final look up and down, he lit a cigarette, walked quickly to the Chevrolet and backed it a hundred yards up the road.

Then, steering carefully, he accelerated down towards the recumbent figure in the dust.

Chapter 3

Up-Country Girls

AFTER THE COMFORTABLE red earth of the coffee country and the alternating woods and escarpments of Minas Gerais state, the plateau on which Brasilia is built seemed almost indecently bare. Solo leaned his forehead against the cool double glass and scanned the bleak terrain sliding past below the plane's wing. Threads of silver splashed the ravines here and there, and way off to the northeast a wide, shallow river coiled itself between trees. But there was nothing he could see that suggested in any way the building of a new dam or an artificial lake.

The smart young corporation lawyer in the government office, his Bahia university degree framed on the peeled sycamore wall behind him, was equally discouraging.

"I cannot imagine how you can have been so misinformed, Senhor Williams," he said with a frown. "Every hydroelectric project connected with Brasilia was completed before life in the town began, naturally. If such a supplementary scheme existed, and if there were options to acquire, be sure that we should know of them. This is a new town, hardly five years old, and there is

25

little here yet but civic and municipal buildings: physically, there is no place for any undercover dealing to go!"

"I understand," Solo said. "I should explain that of course I did not come to Brazil only to explore these options—if they exist—but on another matter entirely. It was just that I heard of them in a roundabout way and thought it might conceivably be worth investigating."

"Quite. You will forgive me—but you are sure that you have the right city?"

The agent grinned suddenly, disarmingly. "No," he said frankly, "to tell you the truth, I'm not, and that's the hell of it!"

"Well, in that case . . ."

"I heard of it from an old man, a countryman—and I was the one who first mentioned Brasilia, thinking this must be the city he meant from his description. You know, white towers rising against a blue sky, the whole modern city bit. But of course he may have agreed just to be polite—the courtesy of your peasants can be exhausting!"

The young lawyer smiled. "Of course the description would fit Getuliana just as well," he murmured.

"Getuliana?"

"Another of our bright new cities—scheduled population of one million, mostly to be employed in light industry, red carpet to be unrolled at the beginning of 1970. But it's still in the steel frame and cement-mixer stage now—and I shouldn't wonder if there weren't some hydroelectric schemes tied up with that."

"Where exactly is this place?"

"Beyond the Sierra Divisoes, about 300 miles from here. It's on the fringe of the Matto Grosso west of Goiás."

"And you think a dam's a possibility in the neighborhood?"

"I wouldn't know. The site's between the Rio Grande and the Rio das Mortes—both of which flow north into the Araquaia—so I should guess so. But the man you want to ask is Moraes: he can tell you everything about Getuliana."

"Moraes?"

"The contractor who pulled off the deal to build the entire city center. If there are options around he'll know where and what they are—and if it would be worth your while to go up there or not."

Dom Federico de Moraes occupied three floors of a concrete polygon situated across a parched square from the government office where Solo had met the young lawyer. A big, gray man with empty eyes, he was sitting behind a teak desk staring at the wall when Solo was ushered in by a pretty Negro secretary.

"You wished to see me about some aspect of the building of Getuliana, Senhor—ah—Williams?" he rumbled, glancing at Solo's card.

"Not precisely, Dom Federico. At least not the city itself. My interest centers rather"—Solo risked a long shot—"on the dam."

"Ah, the San Felipe project!"

"Precisely. The San Felipe project."

"But I cannot see what interest that can have for an American. Especially an American lawyer."

"One had been informed—perhaps wrongly—that there might be land options negotiable on the fringes of the site, in areas cleared but not inundated. The corporation I represent would be interested in such options . . . either for development or simply for the mineral rights."

A door shut softly behind a dividing screen of potted plants. A tall, thin man in a white suit sauntered into the room. "Oh, sorry, Moraes," he said. "I didn't realize you had company." But he made no attempt to leave, dropping into a tan leather armchair shaped like half a golf ball and staring at Solo with unabashed curiosity.

"It's all right, Wassermann," Moraes said. "This gentleman has been sent here under a misapprehension. He seems to think there are some options available in connection with San Felipe!" He chuckled throatily.

"Options?" The thin man sat upright, his tanned, skull-like face a mask of incredulity. "At San Felipe? You must be joking! May I ask exactly where you got that idea, sir?"

"In Rio."

The two men exchanged glances over the desk. "But I'm afraid I don't understand," the contractor said. "There never have been any options available in connection with this project. The whole thing is what you Americans call a package deal. Doctor Wassermann here conceived the whole idea of building the city and opening up this barren area, persuaded the government to give him the go-ahead, raised the necessary finance in Europe and elsewhere, and negotiated the contracting deal—for everything, absolutely everything—with my company. The dam at San Felipe is simply to provide electricity for the city; that is all."

"One would be interested to learn who gave you the idea," the man in the white suit pursued. "We are more than adequately financed; we do not want your American dollars here. Nothing personal—but you can't buy your way in everywhere, you know."

Solo inclined his head. "Accepted, gentlemen," he said. "That was not my intention. It was just that I heard of the possibility of options and I considered it—foolishly, as it turns out—worth the visit to investigate."

"Yes, but heard from *whom*," Wasserman insisted. "There has been very little publicity—mainly because the whole project *is* being handled by one concern—and I'm amazed it's a talking point in Rio at all."

"A woman, actually," Solo said, deciding to trail a line in deep waters. "A woman who works for the D.A.M.E.S. . . . at San Felipe."

Again the two businessmen exchanged glances. "Ah, the welfare ladies!" Moraes said smoothly after a moment. "Yes, of course. They are engaged in—er—resettling the natives displaced by the new lake. Although that part of the Matto Grosso plateau is relatively bare, a big reservoir such as the one formed by the San Felipe dam is bound to drown quite a few villages and farms in the valley it fills up. The D.A.M.E.S. has been most helpful in explaining to the country folk how they will benefit, and smoothing out the task of rehousing them elsewhere."

"And, apparently, setting up an unofficial agency for

the disposal of our land!" Wassermann remarked dryly.

"I think you exaggerate a little, senhor," Solo said easily. "The lady did not specifically offer land for sale or state that options were available. She merely mentioned the area of operations, as it were, and said in passing that she guessed there must be a lot of money to be made by anyone who could get in on the ground floor. As that happens to be my business, I thought it worth coming to see, as I said."

"How very curious," Wassermann drawled. He rose suddenly to his feet, the elegant suit, creaseless and immaculate, bright in the shadowed office. "There are many ladies of this organization at San Felipe. Do you by any chance recall the name of the one you talked to?"

"At the moment," Solo said, looking him it the eye, "I'm afraid it escapes me."

"I see. Permit me, then, to save you any further trouble in this connection. You may take it from me that the dam, which has inundated a valley carrying a tributary of the Rio das Mortes, is in a stretch of country wild and inaccessible. Most of the rocks are ancient porphyries, of no value for mining, building or any other work. Apart from San Felipe do Caiapo itself—a village of three or four hundred people only—there are no centers of population nearer than the unfinished city. Nor are there likely to be, since there are no roads. And nor will there be any question whatever of land or mineral options."

"Nevertheless, since you use the services of the D.A.M.E.S., you must in some degree be prepared to work with Americans. The trust is wholly American-financed, you know."

"That is hardly a parallel. They provide a service we need. By contributing to their funds *we*, in effect, pay *them*. Which is a bit different from accepting money from those wishing to share our future profits!"

"Admittedly. Even so, as a businessman—"

"Good day, Mr. Williams."

And that was that. Solo cut his losses and left. He had found out more than he had dared to hope for: there *was* a dam and a reservoir; he knew now where it was.

There *was* a team of D.A.M.E.S. working at it—or at least a team of women representing themselves as the D.A.M.E.S.; and this was undoubtedly where the two girls murdered in Rio had come from. The people working on the project were the same people making the new town; and it seemed fairly certain they wanted to keep their activities secret.

Why?

What was there about another new town in Brazil—even if there might have been graft attached to the dispensation of the contracts for doing it—that was so special?

There was only one way to find out, Solo thought: go there.

Picking his way between slender, modernistic pillars supporting the giant canopies designed to keep the sun off the inhabitants of Brasilia, he threaded his way across the new city. Within the plane-shaped overall design of the place, squares, gardens, parking lots, shadowed pedestrian walks, and the geometric forms of buildings merged into a homogeneous whole that was as stimulating as it was right. Here was the city of the future before his eyes. And yet the very perfection of the place rendered it sterile and somehow un-alive. It had sprung into being straight off the drawing board, without being allowed to develop from older and more traditional failures that were there before. And perhaps because of this, it was with a sense of relief that he saw the car-rental headquarters was hewn from a different block. It was an unholy mixture of adobe and corrugated iron, a series of long walls topped with rule-of-thumb roofs linked by the French truss method. The office was a wooden shack shoveled into a corner behind a double row of Plymouths. And to Solo it looked like home.

He burst in through the rickety door and flipped a silver coin at the young Brazilian equivalent of a New York radio cab dispenser who sat behind the worn counter. "I need to rent a car," he said. "Now."

" 'Kay, bud," the dispenser said, rolling a toothpick from side to side of his mouth. "Where you wanna go?"

"Does it matter?" Solo asked, a little surprised both at the question and at the fact that it was couched in archaic Hollywood English.

"Well sure it matters, bud. Like if you was to wanna drive to Januaria, or Claros, or Rio Branco in Bahia state, then I give you a Plymouth, see. It's a long ways there, first-off, and then again the roads ain't too bad. Same thing if you was mad enough to wanna go to the railhead at Pirapora. But if you just had a mind to drive around here, maybe go up to Palma, down to Carvalhas, I'd suggest something smaller, cheaper on the gas. A Volvo, maybe, or a Fiat. 'Cause it's flat up here. On the other hand, if you were heading for Leopoldina or Goiania or any of those places, you'd be better off with a jeep. Those roads in the mountains are rugged, man."

"I want to go to Getuliana."

"Getuliana!"

"Sure. If you don't mind. Bud."

"Jesus! What you wanna do that for?"

"I'd like to see it, that's all. Anything wrong with that?"

"Only that it ain't there. There's nothing to see. You go to the public library here, you can see the *plans*. Look around this dump, and you can see the way it's *going* to be. But out at the site, you won't see nothing. It's like this place but less so, if you know what I mean."

"Even so, I'd like to take a run out there and look. I'm interested in town planning."

"Yeah, sure. So am I. But an interest can turn into an *obsession*. . . . Look, lemme tell you about a great trip you can take down the valley—"

"Thanks, but it has to be Getuliana. I'm being paid for it."

"Well, if you're sure," the youth said doubtfully. "I guess you better take the Volkswagen, then. She ain't pretty, she ain't specially fast, she's not what you call *comfortable*—but she's tough, man. Real tough. And she'll save you gas . . . even, God save us, on the roads around Getuliana!"

"Great. I'll take the VW, then. Maybe you could help me work out a route, eh? You have maps here?"

"Maps we got, bud. The road system in Bahia state.

31

The road system in Minas Cerais. The trunk routes of Rio. The river system of Brazil. Tributaries of the Amazon. How to make the best of our railway network. Street maps of Brasilia—lots of those, in all colors, with electricity and drainage diagrams added. But a map that shows how to get from here to Getuliana . . ." He shook his head. "Man, that's a drag."

"Do you know the way yourself? You've been there, I mean?"

"Sure. I been there a couple times. But I ain't no chauffeur."

"Understood. I just meant that maybe you could kind of show me the general way on that big wall map you have there." Solo gestured towards a six-foot plaster mural in exaggerated relief which dominated one wall of the office.

"Pleasure, if that's all you want. . . . You head west across the plateau here, see . . . practically desert all the way. Then you have to get through the Pireneos—that's this ridge here—and cross the Divisoes. After that, watch out."

"Hostile natives?"

The boy looked at him suspiciously. "This is a modern country, bud," he said. "You have to watch out for the roads. You'll see signs directing you to the grand new autoroute for Leopoldina and Getuliana."

"And the road's not built yet?"

"Oh, it's there all right. Only they haven't put in the bridges where it crosses these valleys, see . . . here . . . and here . . . and here. You have to take the old road—but only as far as this junction here. There's a big old church right between the two roads; you can't miss it. When you get there, turn off that road and head southwest."

"No bridges on the old road either?"

"Oh, there were bridges, sure. Only they got kinda washed away in the rainy season and they're not fixed up again yet. . . . Look, you'd best head for Goiás from there. It's further south, but the road's much better. Then you can strike north along this valley, cross the saddle here, and come down on Getuliana from the

32

other side, through San Felipe—you'll recognize that because there's a big new lake and a dam there."

Solo made a few notes and completed the necessary insurance and financial details before the boy led him out to a bright blue Volkswagen, slightly battered around the fenders but otherwise in good condition.

"Like I say, she's tough," the boy said. "And she's got plenty of ground clearance in there. But it rains, you wanna watch out for that back end, man . . . like especially where they're mining that bauxite."

"Thanks," Solo said, pressing another coin into his hand. "I guess maybe you get them late down here, huh?"

"How's that?"

"The movies. They're on pretty late release here, eh? . . . I mean, you ought to know this: *On the Waterfront* was a long time ago. Brando is out now. Not the in thing at all."

"He's not?"

"Definitely not. The in thing today is to get all British. Frightfully proper, what! Clipped voice and school English; high collar with a tie. Buttoned down. The whole scene."

"You're kidding!"

"Absolutely not, dear boy. Hadn't you noticed *my* collar?"

Solo was still grinning when he swung the Volkswagen onto the main road to the west outside the city limits. Allowing for detours, he had over three hundred miles to go. Since it was already past noon, he would be wiser not to press for too much: he would stop for the night at Goiás and prospect San Felipe and the dam tomorrow.

The road plunged across the empty countryside in wide sweeps, now smooth and hard-packed, now pitted, rough and covered with a layer of choking white dust. Once through the jagged rock defile breaching the first ridge, it ran gradually downhill and the spiny plants of the desert gave way to a denser vegetation. Soon the car was bowling through the middle of a forest, shaded from the fiery sun by a palisade of tall trees. Green parakeets swooped and soared in flocks, and an occasional pair of toucans flapped heavily from one side of the road to the other.

Traffic was light. In an hour, Solo saw only three cars, a jeep, the inevitable rattletrap bus, and a convoy of heavy trucks loaded with something in steel drums which he had to wait some time to pass.

Then the forest receded, was replaced by ragged bush, and finally gave way to a plain of tufted grasses bounded by hills violet with distance to the west. Halfway across the plain was the fork with a church between the two roads, just as the boy at the rental company had said. Ignoring the signposts, Solo turned left and found himself a quarter of an hour later in an arid region gushed with dried-up watercourses The road appeared to be quarried from the bed-rock, the dust billowed into the air and penetrated the car in choking clouds, and both fabrics and metal became too hot to touch in the shadeless glare of the sun. Several times Solo had to drive across *mataburros*—the primitive country bridges comprising two steel beams spanning the gap, with a series of planks laid crosswise to form the roadway. Once, finding himself stranded on one of these high above a desolate gorge, he had to stop the car, get out, collect an armful of planks from behind and lay them down again in front of the car to fill in a space in the swaying structure before he could go on. Another time, he missed a turn-off and found himself—according to a signpost—on the way back to Brasilia. It was after dark before he finally made Goiás.

The following morning—he had gone straight to bed after an inn dinner of *feijao* with eggs and roast meat, washed down by strong coffee laced with *pinga*—Solo decided he must get in touch with Waverly to report progress. But first he wanted to ask a few questions of the locals. . . .

He went out into the town to look around.

It was another hot day, the sun blazing from a dark blue sky between drifts of white cloud. The town was pleasant, a survival from an earlier age. There was a

34

river, a square with green turf and a bandstand presided over by a peeling building like a Venetian *palazzo*, a movie theater with an ornate facade. There were narrow cobbled streets twisting awry the rules of perspective. And above the jumbled roofs with their curved tiles, wooded hills surmounted by a wild rock escarpment pierced the sky.

Against the blinding white walls of the house, men in wide straw hats tipped back their chairs and drowsed. From inside, occasionally, the age-old profile of a woman gleamed pale against the shadow.

Solo threaded his way through a market, enjoying the spicy smells in the shade beneath the awnings, and crossed a square loud with the clatter of small boys on ponies. On the far side, over the ever-present babble of the river, he heard a low murmur of men's voices from a window below street level. He went down half a dozen steps, pushed open a wrought iron gate, and found himself in a *bodega*.

It was moist and cool after the glare of the sun, and the low-pitched conversation blended well with the woody smells of barrel and cask. Solo ran his eyes over the double line of spigots behind the counter, each with its neat label, and approached the barman.

"I'll take a *sercial*, if you please," he said, "providing it's chilled but not too cold."

Although he spoke Portuguese well, it was some time before Solo was able to break down the mistrust of strangers sufficiently to take part in the general conversation. Finally, however, as he started to sip his third glass of the dry, clean-tasting Madeira, he found himself sitting down with three men at a heavy, polished table, talking of local trade. One of the men was a wholesaler of groceries and dry goods.

"I suppose you will find a big difference, now that they are building the new city," Solo said. "More clients will mean bigger orders of stock, and larger stocks will need larger premises and so on."

The man gave a short laugh. "Getuliana?" he said. "The new city? *When* they build it—*if* they build it—I may have to consider such things. But at the moment that is very much a thing of the future."

"They will never build it," a fat fruit farmer said mournfully.

"If you ask me," the third man, a pharmacist with drooping moustaches, put in, "they never intended to build the place. It's just a way for businessmen in the capital to chisel money out of the government."

"It is not completed, then?" Solo asked innocently.

"Getuliana completed?" the pharmacist exploded. "That would be the day, senhor! The site is flattened and streets are marked out. They say some power cables and drains are down. But not one stone has been laid upon another . . ."

"Even the machines have departed," the farmer said. "There are a few bulldozers left, a handful of trucks, and one crane, I think."

"Window dressing!" the wholesaler snorted. "To make the people think the work proceeds. In truth only the dispensation of money proceeds—while the contractors and their lawyers disport themselves at Copacabana and Sao Paulo and Bahia. Maybe even at Brasilia."

"But I thought the new dam . . . One had heard . . ."

"Ah, the San Felipe dam: that is a different matter. For some reason they have got a move on there. They have been working—"

"That is just what I mean," the pharmacist interrupted. "Not a house is built in the city, yet already the hydro-electric scheme is finished, thousands of hectares of land drowned, thousands of people made homeless, and nowhere for the electricity to go! This is town planning?"

"You are right, Humberto. It is madness."

"I do not agree," the farmer said. "If—I say if—the city is ever to be built, surely it is prudent to have the electricity ready beforehand—then they can use the power to help build the place!"

"No, no. You miss the point . . ."

"One must consider the dispossessed peasants . . ."

"I thought"—Solo in turn interrupted, struggling for a foothold in the discussion—"I thought those displaced from their land and their homes by the new reservoir

36

had been resettled with the aid of this American missionary body."

"Resettled? *Unsettled*, more likely," the wholesaler said. "Those women, I suppose you mean? The ones in the uniforms?"

"Well, yes. But—"

"This is a Catholic country, senhor. Admittedly most of the people resettled were either Indians—the Carajas—or country Negroes who worship at their own Candomble. Even so, the susceptibilities of the population as a whole must be considered."

"You cloak the truth with words, Miguel. The fact of the matter is that these women behave in a manner likely to offend anyone, anywhere."

"I'm afraid I don't understand," Solo said. "The society —the D.A.M.E.S., it is called—is ultra-respectable. Whenever their members are stationed abroad, they have to live in special hostels and follow a set of rigid behavior rules. What exactly is being complained of here?"

"Drunken singing far into the night, indecent behavior with the men from the site, reckless driving on the roads, unseemly dress—anything you like."

"But this is astonishing," Solo said. "For an organization so well considered . . ."

"It astonished us, too, senhor. You will not take the criticism personally as an American, I hope. But San Felipe do Caiapo is a very small village."

"I understand. Perhaps the women will go away when the dam is completed and leave the villagers in peace."

"Perhaps. But it is already finished, I believe."

"You do not know? Is it not a remarkable thing that people drive out to see, this man-made lake?"

The pharmacist laughed. "The road from Goiás to Leopoldina is reputed to be the worst in Brazil," he said. "Halfway along it, there turns off the road to San Felipe —and this makes the Leopoldina road seem like one of your superhighways! From here to the dam is almost seventy miles—and over the second half of the journey it is impossible to average ten miles per hour."

"Also," the farmer said, "those building the dam and the power station by the *barrage* actively discourage vis-

37

itors, it seems. Besides, it is high in the bare hills and the road, such as it is, follows the lower ground."

"But surely there must be many trucks, convoys of trucks, taking materials to the site?"

"Not through Goiás. We see a few—mainly hauliers from the coast carrying Brazilian goods from Volta Redondas: oil and chemicals and that sort of thing. There are others bringing stuff south from the river at Leopoldina; they offload it from the boats there. But the bulk of it is flown in to the strip at Getuliana, of course."

"I see. . . . Gentlemen! Your glasses are empty. With what may it be my pleasure to fill them?" Solo said, laughing. "And there is certainly one place, after our conversation, that you *won't* find me visiting while I'm in this part of the country!"

Nevertheless, it was towards the road to Leopoldina and San Felipe that he headed the Volkswagen as soon as he could decently leave.

The clouds had vanished and the startling blue of the sky was unbroken save for the shapes of vultures soaring over the gables of Goiás. Napoleon Solo hung his jacket on a hanger from the loop behind the front seat, loosened his collar, rolled up his sleeves and prepared for a long, difficult and intensely hot journey.

It was nearly ten o'clock at night when he returned. As soon as the dusty car turned the last bend and came in sight of the scattered lights of the town below, he pulled off the road and cut the motor. From the luggage space in the VW's front, he removed a pigskin case—and from the case he took a pair of silver backed brushes, a safety razor, a manicure set and a bottle of toilet water with an ornate stopper. Each of these articles could be dismantled, and from the interior of each came an assortment of precision parts which could be assembled into a miniature radio transceiver. It took the agent two and a quarter minutes to set up the gear, another thirty seconds to dismantle the car aerial and refit it in a special socket at one side of the set, and nine minutes of patient fiddling with dials and knobs and tuners before he heard an answer to his call-sign on the wavelength he was using.

He picked up the tiny microphone, thumbed the button on its side and spoke softly. "Hello, Recife?" he said. "Is that Da Costa at Recife? . . . Are you hearing me loud and clear? . . . Please acknowledge and advise. Over."

Releasing the button, he lifted a small earphone, flicked a diminutive switch and craned his head to one side, listening to the tinny sounds within the can.

"Okay," he said at length, resuming the microphone and throwing the switch once more. "I'm not going to dictate you a message for passing on to Waverly. You know the procedure. It'll read oddly because you are to send it in clear—do you understand? It is to go in clear, for political reasons. Message begins: Following are certs and probables for Brazilian Hit Parade . . ."

Half an hour later, he was running the Volkswagen in under the eaves of the huge barn which acted as garage for the inn. Hardly a light showed in the shuttered streets; there was more illumination from a sky prickled out with stars than was offered to the municipality of Goiás as he stumbled across the yard and in at the back door of the hotel.

Once in his room, he checked methodically the half dozen tiny personal signposts that every agent leaves to tip him off in case of entry or search. Of the five cigarettes in the pack carelessly thrown on the table, three still had the brand names on the paper facing downwards. The corner of the folded map on the bureau still coincided with the angle of a letter V in the title of a book below it. Nothing had disturbed the irregularly shaped morsel of flint he had balanced on top of one of the drawers. He poured himself a glass of water from the carafe, pulled his sticky shirt over his head, and continued. The suitcase came next: carefully he eased open the catches. Balanced on a stud-box inside was a small pile of coins. The top one should be a 1936 Spanish peseta with the first numeral of the date pointing at the top left-hand corner of the case.

It was.

Solo sighed with relief. It looked as though the place was clean, all right. Not that he expected anything, but you could never relax. He would just check the last three pointers and then he could get to bed. First, though, he must have another drink and get the rest of his clothes off. It really was tremendously hot tonight.

He was staring straight at the ceiling then. He couldn't think why, for the moment, and then he realized that he was lying on his back on the floor. He had no recollection of having fallen, and no time seemed to have elapsed since he had formed the thought about the closeness of the night. It was very odd.

He got up, shaking his head, and reached for the glass of water. At least some of it was left—and he was exceedingly thirsty.

The floor spun away to his left and the bed moved in and hit him on the shoulder. He opened his mouth but no sound came out of it. The religious pictures on the wall advanced and receded in a blur of movement.

And then suddenly, in a blinding moment of clarity, he had it: of course they hadn't bothered to search his things or turn over his luggage. Why bother when you can drug a man's drinking water on a hot night—and then search to your heart's content without arousing his . . . without arousing his what? . . . It was too dark to remember.

Desperately, Solo struggled to a sitting position. *Idiot, idiot, idiot,* a voice screamed into his dwindling consciousness. *For a professional to be caught by such a trick . . .*

He clawed at the bed but his fingers were swollen and woolly. The counterpane whirled away into the stars as the night burst through the wall. Dimly, he sensed the presence of people, of figures moving in a mist.

And then something exploded with a soft, almost caressing flare in his head, and he began to fall. . . .

Chapter 4

A Matter of Interpretation

ICY RAIN lanced across the East River and rattled on the window of Alexander Waverly's office as a squall hurled itself on the city from the north. Outside the shabby block sheathing the electronic complexities of U.N.C.L.E. from a curious world, people turned up the collars of their raincoats and hurried to get in off the glistening street. A young man wrestled with an umbrella that had blown inside out on the sidewalk by Del Floria's tailor shop.

Waverly himself faced a woman across the immensity of his desk. Apart from the low humming of the air-conditioning, there was silence in the room. At length, the woman gave a short sigh of exasperation and shrugged her plump shoulders. "All right, Alexander, if you *insist* on being so conscientious, I suppose I'll have to accept it . . . but I think you're being unnecessarily obstructive. As Commandant of the D.A.M.E.S., surely I have a right to—"

"Barbara! Please!" Waverly interrupted. "There are no 'rights' at all in this matter. And I'm not being over-scrupulous at all."

"I didn't say that. I said obstructive. And I think—"

"You meant that. But the point is simply this: we happen to have come across a case where, in another country, some women have been claiming to be members of your organization. The circumstances surrounding that case are of interest to us, so we are investigating it. Because the women are actually *not* members of your body, naturally you are interested too. You want to know why. But that does not give you the right to demand information about the case as a whole, or to be made party to the confidential reports of my operatives. Indeed, I'm very surprised that you should ask."

"Oh, Alexander, don't be so stuffy! You know perfectly well what I mean: I simply want to know, to put it in a nutshell, what it's all about. That's all."

"And to vulgarize my own position, Barbara, the answer is that I simply cannot tell you. I haven't the right to. All I can say, if it's any help, is that the fact they chose *your* organization as a cover is practically coincidental."

"I'm delighted. But what I want to know—"

"The case we're investigating, quite literally, has nothing whatever to do with you. Nothing."

"Since you have interrupted me three times in the

41

past two minutes, I gather that's as much as you are prepared to say. But I warn you, Alexander—I'll take the
matter further. We do have friends in the Pentagon."

Waverly rose to his feet. He was smiling good-natur-
edly. "By all means, Barbara, pull all the strings you can,"
he said equably. "And if you come across anything really
succulent, let me know, won't you?"

Mrs. Stretford rose too—five foot four inches of effi-
ciency tightly swathed in the green tweed of the D.A.
M.E.S. military-style uniform. "You can joke as much as
you like," she said briskly, settling the hat with its gold-
starred cockade and upturned brim more firmly above
her clear eyes and ruddy cheeks. "But you know I have
a way of getting things done."

Waverly merely smiled. He reached for a pipe, discovered that it was already stuffed with unsmoked tobacco, and groped in his pocket for another. As soon as
the creak of Barbara Stretford's sensible brogues had
died away across the anteroom, he thumbed the button
on his desk and called: "Have Mr. Kuryakin come in
now, if you please."

Illya Nickovetch Kuryakin had been born in Russia—
a fact that the international organization employing him
occasionally found useful, especially when they were
working in cooperation with Warsaw Pact powers. Beneath a high forehead fringed with pale hair, his eyes,
blue and deep-set, regarded the world of his adoption
with a seriousness that was alternately the stimulation
and the exasperation of the young women who worked
in the U.N.C.L.E. headquarters. He lived in a small
bachelor apartment in Brooklyn Heights, he was a good
lab man, a mine of information on the latest electronic
advances, an expert on firearms and radio. And he was
also, with Napoleon Solo, one of the two Enforcement
Agents Waverly rated highest on his private list.

"My apologies for keeping you waiting, Mr. Kuryakin," Waverly said now as he motioned Illya to a chair
on the far side of his desk. "I have been doing battle with
Commandant Stretford, the D.A.M.E.S. lady. If only she
realized how little—how very little—we know about

her precious Brazilian, ah, bombshells!"

"You have heard no more from Napoleon?"

"Nothing. Just the one radio message forwarded by Recife. Not a word since . . . and that was the morning of the day before yesterday."

"Maybe he found himself on a promising trail and hasn't been able to find time to get through again. Were you definitely expecting him to call back?"

"Yes, we were. On his own instructions, too. He told our man in Recife to listen at the same time the following evening, to be sure he didn't miss out on a transmission he expected to be very important."

Kuryakin's quiet blue-gray eyes rested steadily on Waverly for a long moment before he said softly, "I see what you mean."

"I don't like it. I don't like it at all," Waverly said. "It's not like Mr. Solo to make an arrangment and fail to keep it. Something must have happened to him. The question is—what? If only he had been able to be more explicit in his message. . . ."

"Was it in clear or in code, Mr. Waverly?"

"Oh, didn't I show it to you? Here. . . ." Waverly picked up a piece of paper from his desk and passed it across. "It's kind of half and half, as you see. I told him not to send anything in code or cypher, because we can't run the risk of offending the Brazilians by sending secret messages out of their country without telling them we're operating there. You never know when a regular post might be monitored. On the other hand, he couldn't very well put down chapter and verse in clear. So he's done it in plain English—but we have to interpret the meaning." He smiled frostily as Kuryakin put on a pair of glasses and read the message:

FOLLOWING ARE CERTS AND PROBABLES FOR BRAZILIAN HIT PARADE STOP CERTS THE LADY IS A TRAMP STOP REPEAT STOP REPEAT STOP DAM YANKEES STOP UP THE LAZY RIVER STOP I'M GONNA GO FISHING STOP HELP BY THE BEETLES STOP PROBABLES STARS FELL ON ALABAMA STOP OUT

OF NOWHERE STOP HERNANDO'S HIDEA-
WAY STOP UNCLE TOM'S CABIN STOP BIRD-
BRAIN STOP SECOND TEN PROWAVERLY TO-
MORROW STOP EXOLO.

"Well?" Waverly inquired as Kuryakin looked up.

"Not too easy," the Russian admitted. "I take it the
technique of using a popular song Hit Parade is merely
a device to provide reason for having a number of unusual images all together, rather than a lead in itself?"

Waverly nodded.

"Then we have ten songs listed—five under certs and
five under probables. May we assume these are simply
facts and conjectures, respectively?"

Again Waverly inclined his head. "That's the way I
see it," he said.

"Good. Now, first of all, why the two repeats in the
first entry? I cannot understand that at all."

"Simply, I think, to make the title plural. Several ladies. In other words, he confirms that there are spurious
D.A.M.E.S., none of whom are—as my mother used to
say—any better than they should be."

"Then obviously he is saying later that he is going to
investigate somewhere—going fishing. Though where the
lazy river is, I don't know. There are several water images . . . Oh." He paused and looked at Waverly. "I see
the 'Damn' of *Damn Yankees* is spelled wrong. Would
that be deliberate?"

"It would. Recife said he was insistent on triple-
checking all the spelling."

"Ah. Could the river perhaps be lazy *because* of a
dam, then?"

"It's a possibility—though what it has to do with
Yankees, I cannot see."

"Let's leave that for a moment, then, and pass to the
last factual one. He needs help—but why put in the
artists, when he hasn't before, and again, why misspell
the Beatles?"

"There's a reason," Waverly said. "We'll come to it
later. In the meantime, what do you make of the second
five?"

"Stars fell on Alabama out of nowhere—that's a frightening image," Illya said thoughtfully. "Especially when you connect it with the last entry."

"The last entry?"

"A minor Charlie Parker piece. Not well know even among his fans—and in quite a different category from the rest, all of which are big, number one best-sellers of one era or another."

"Yes. I thought it odd too. He must have included it because that number, and only that one, perfectly expressed his meaning. What do you make of it?"

"In our business, bird connected with brain can mean only one thing," Kuryakin said soberly.

"Exactly."

"And if he has stumbled on some plot of Thrush's—and they've caught him—his chances must be very slim," the Russian continued. "Mr. Waverly—I'd like you to assign me to go and get him out. I'm used to working with him, I know the methods he uses and therefore I can backtrack on him more easily. "

"That is true. Very well—but please disabuse your mind of any romantic ideas of 'going in to get him out.' In the first place, we do not know for sure (a) whether it is in fact Thrush, and (b) whether there may not be some perfectly innocent explanation for his silence. Secondly, we do not in either case know for sure that he's 'in.' And thirdly, the requirements of the assignment —which naturally overrule personal consideration—may call for you to play a waiting game."

"But, Mr. Waverly—"

"The job, Mr. Kuryakin, comes before anything else. Surely you of all my operatives are aware of that?"

"Yes, sir."

"Good. To recap, then: you will go to Rio de Janeiro and pick up Mr. Solo's trail there. We know from his previous messages through Recife that he was using the name of Williams and the cover of a lawyer. We know that he spoke to a police captain named Garcia, and the two women he wished to interview were murdered in their beds, and that after visiting the site of the car crash, he returned to Rio and took the first available plane to Brasilia. The rest, as a great Englishman said, is silence."

"Very good, sir. Before following him to Brasilia, I had better try and find out what caused him to go. It will prove quicker in the long run, I think."

"I agree," Waverly said dryly. "But I am afraid you may be too late." He handed the agent a photostat.

It was a copy of a circled news item from a two-days-old Rio paper. It was headed DEATH STRIKES TWICE AT FATAL CURVE and it read:

The body of Miguel Oliveira, 73, retired fruit farmer of Santa Maria da Conceicao, was discovered yesterday afternoon on a mountain road outside the city at the very place where two American women were involved three days ago in a fatal accident when their car left the highway. The old man, who traversed the route every day, is thought to have dismounted from his mule for some reason and suffered at the hands of a hit-and-run driver.

"They—whoever they are—are nothing if not thorough," Waverly continued. "I wouldn't take any bets on whether or not that old man provided the reason for Mr. Solo's sudden decision to go to Brasilia. With him *and* the girls dead, you're left with no definite lead at all."

"Yes. I notice the paper said nothing about the women having been murdered."

"No. The Brazilian police are touchy about people who get killed in their care. They preferred to let readers infer the girls died as a result of the accident."

"I see. There is just a slim chance, then, that our villains may not realize quite how much we know or have guessed about them?"

"I suppose so, yes."

"Good. I'll go to the armory and draw my PPK, then, and call in on Operations for a full briefing on my way back."

"Very well, Mr. Kuryakin. You may liaise with the Brazilian police to the extent that you may overtly be looking for a colleague, Mr. Williams, the lawyer, who seems unaccountably to have disappeared."

"And my liaison with you?"

"Don't call me," Waverly said, superbly unconscious of paraphrasing: "I shall call you. . . . I don't want to overload the radio traffic from Recife any more. Leave it to me to get in touch with you, and you can report as and when contacted. No doubt you will find the reference to *Uncle Tom's Cabin* and *Hernando's Hideaway* perfectly explicit once you are on the scene."

"No doubt," Illya said. "I'll see you at Philippi, then."

His chief looked up sharply. "Philippi?" he queried. "Where's that? Or what's that?"

"It's the Greek for Sevastopol," Illya said softly as he closed the door from the outside.

He went to the armory and drew his gun and several smaller and more recondite devices, called in at Operations, went to the Library to read the secret files on the case so far, took the elevator down past the warren of the Communications section to the street level, and walked into the entrance foyer. From here, monitored by closed-circuit TV, four exits led from the building: one via the top floor of the restaurant-club at one end of the block; another through the public garage at the far end; a third by way of a subterranean channel cut through from the river; and the last, reserved for operating agents, via a concealed door in a changing cubicle at the back of Del Floria's tailor shop. Kuryakin handed in the triangular yellow badge that had permitted him to rise to Waverly's floor, said "Good-day" expressionlessly to the ex-West Indian beauty queen presiding at the desk, and walked through into the cubicle.

Outside the steamed-up windows of the shop, the rain had stopped and a hundred sections of dripping guttering above the brownstones played an obbligato to the mournful swish of tires on the wet street. But there was still hardly a soul about. The young man with the inside-out umbrella—he had finally junked it in a trash baket—had no difficulty in following Illya Kuryakin at all.

47

Chapter 5

Old Wine In New Bottles!

In Rio de Janeiro, Illya Kuryakin met with a blank wall of official silence—not because the authorities wished to impede his investigation, but because Solo, after all, had been working strictly alone and they had nothing to tell him. About the murdered girls, police headquarters were polite but noncommittal. It was a murder case, they were handling it in their own way, and since he had no official standing they were giving nothing away. In the district bureau, Captain Garcia was equally courteous—and equally vague. The Senhor Williams had come to the hospital, learned the tragic news, accompanied the captain back to his office and talked for a while, and then left. It was true that patrolmen Da Silva and Gomez had seen his hired car parked near the site of the accident—what he had wanted there, the Captain could not think—but that was not against the law and anyway he had come straight back to the city, returned the rented Buick, and left by plane for Brasilia shortly after. So far as the old man killed by the hit-and-run driver was concerned, the police were disposed to dismiss it as a coincidence. There was, it was true, the slight—the million to one—chance that the old man had been deliberately killed to stop him revealing something he had told the Senhor Williams in a conversation. It was an interesting possibility, and one that the police would keep in mind. . . .

It was the same thing at the hotel. The gentleman had checked in, stayed the night, eaten elsewhere, spent a second night there, called for his bill, paid, and left by the early morning plane to Brasilia. He had given them no forwarding address.

At a public library near the hotel, a clerk recognized a photo of the missing agent, and said that he had been consulting topographical maps of the country. He had himself recommended him to go to the bureau of public

48

works if he wished to inform himself more closely. Something to do with a projected dam or a hydroelectric scheme, he thought. . . .

The car rental company could add nothing to the details of the short transaction that Illya already knew. A lawyer had hired a Buick and returned it the following day having done less than a hundred miles. Period.

He was walking disconsolately back to the hotel, wondering what possible lead he could follow up next, when he halted in mid-stride as he was passing a barbership. It must be a coincidence, it was not possible, it was a trick of hearing . . . but he could have sworn that, through the bead curtain masking the doorway, he had caught an echo from the past, a voice from the dead. He shook his head, his lips creased in a wry little smile, and he was about to go on when he heard the voice again. There was no mistaking it: it *did* sound exactly like . . . On an impulse, he swept aside the curtain and peered into the somber interior of the small shop.

There were only four chairs, ranged before their basins and mirrors in one of the world's most universal patterns. Two of them were untended. The third, at the far end, cradled a recumbent figure swathed in steaming towels with a white-coated barber, beyond, busied about a cupboard of shining instruments. The nearest chair was empty—but beside it was a wheelchair holding an enormous man, a man so vast that he overflowed the big carriage on all sides and towered above the shining steel rails of its back, a man so fat that the swell of his belly almost covered his knees and his bright blue, humorous eyes were nearly lost among the rolls of flesh forming his face. Half submerged in lather, the head topping this great bulk sported a few strands of reddish hair which were combed across the freckled scalp. From a cavern opening and closing in the middle of the foam rumbled the voice whose characteristic tones had first arrested Illya outside the shop.

"And be sure, Pedro me boy, to glide your implement neatly around the spot at the base of me chin—for if you decapitate it again, I'll sure as hell be provoked into

49

leapin' out of this chair at all, and wrappin' your razor around your Brazilian nut," he was saying amiably to the barber shaving him.

"Si, senhor," the hairdresser began, when he was rudely interrupted by Kuryakin, who surged past in a rare moment of exuberance to exclaim:

"Tufik! I knew I couldn't be mistaken: I'd know that County Cork accent anywhere! What in the world are you doing in Rio? You're supposed to be dead!"

The eyes in the great moon face remained closed. Not a muscle twitched beneath the lather. Eventually the hole opened again and the voice said quietly, "County Waterford, as it happens, in the locality of Lismore. But you have the advantage of me, sir—besides which you appear to have made a mistake, for the name by which you greeted me is not my own."

Kuryakin followed the lead instinctively. "I'm so very sorry," he said at once. "I thought it was a friend I hadn't seen for years. Now that my eyes are accustomed to the light, I see I was wrong. My apologies for disturbing you." He smiled deprecatingly at the barber and went out.

Ten minutes later the fat man in the wheelchair was lifted through the bead curtain onto the sidewalk and propelled himself rapidly away on the shadowed side of the street. Kuryakin waited in the shelter of a doorway to an apartment building until he turned into a narrow alley, and then crossed the road and caught up with him.

"Sorry for letting my mouth get the better of me," he said quietly, walking along behind the chair. "I was so surprised to see you that I couldn't stop myself blurting out your name."

"Not to worry, boy," the fat man said without turning his head. "Mr. Kuryakov, isn't it?"

"Kuryakin. Illya Kuryakin."

"To be sure, to be sure. I'll be forgetting me own name next—which by the way is Manuel O'Rourke now. So far as Habib Tufik is concerned—I'd be grateful if *you* would forget that one!"

"Willingly—but what happened? Solo and I heard

that Thrush had blown up your place in Casablanca* and that you had died in the blast. We saw a story in the paper in Alexandria."

"Ah, sure you don't want to believe everything you read in the papers," the Irishman said. "If a feller has good friends—that he's paid well over a period of time, mind—likely it'll happen that they'll tip him off in time to get out while the goin's good, eh?"

Illya nodded with an inward grin. Habib Tufik—as Illya had known him—had been born of an Irish mother and a North African father and had built up over many years an information service in Casablanca that had been without equal in the world. To him, police forces, embassy staff, military attachés, detectives, lawyers, spies and newspapermen from all over the world had come to buy knowledge in the days before Solo and Illya had unwittingly put him on the wrong side of Thrush. His service had been completely impersonal—if clients wanted information, he would supply it . . . at a price. And provided it did not compromise those who were already his clients. His systems of microphone eavesdropping, newspaper "milking," and world-wide cross-indexing, combined with an unrivaled control of hotel porters, liftmen and taxi drivers, had brought him the reputation of the most up-to-date gossip-monger on Earth. Crippled by an early encounter with gangsters whom he had attempted to take on single-handed, he had run his one-man show from his wheelchair, aided only by a handful of loyal strong-arm men.

Until U.N.C.L.E. had involved him with Thrush.

But although his organization had gone, it seemed he had amazingly survived personally the attentions of that evil and ruthless society. And now here he was in South America, complete with new name and personality.

Illya laughed aloud with pleasure at seeing him. "And what exactly are you doing here in Brazil, Senhor . . .

---

*See The Man From U.N.C.L.E. #7, *The Radioactive Camel Affair*.

O'Rourke? And when can you tell me your story?" he asked.

The fat man stopped his chair. "I go in here," he said. "Best not to make it too obvious. Walk on past, you. Then come back in ten minutes. . . . You walk through the iron gates and take the lift. Press the button for the sixteenth."

"The sixteenth?"

"Sure, the penthouse floor. Nothing but the best for yours truly. Thank the dear Lord the Brazilians build wide lifts, eh?"

Illya glanced upwards. True enough, set a little way back from the old, shuttered houses lining the court, the slim pillar of a modern apartment building rose to the sky.

Ten minutes later, he pushed open a wrought-iron ornamental gate and walked down a long, cool passage to a foyer containing a bank of lifts at the far side.

Tufik—or O'Rourke, as Illya now tried to think of him—was waiting in his chair as the doors slid open on the top floor. Spinning the vehicle with all his old expertise, he led the way into a small apartment furnished in ultra-modern style. Beyond a living room bleak with Danish chairs and an angular room divider, a large flagged terrace stretched coolly away beneath a canopy of vines. There were geraniums, salvias, petunias and begonias in pots, and the flanking apartments were shut off by a dense hedge of macrocarpa in green wooden troughs. At the open end of the balcony, a stone balustrade partitioned a jumble of tiled roofs in red and green, beyond which palm trees fringed Copacabana and a vivid blue segment of sea.

"Fantastic!" Illya murmured wonderingly. "For a man in a wheelchair, you certainly manage to fall on your feet, don't you?"

The Irishman chuckled throatily, the pendant folds of flesh masking his chin shaking from side to side. "Ah, sure we manage, we manage," he said. " 'Tis entirely a matter of knowing where to go at the right time . . . plus a little judicious—ah—emolument dispensed over the years, of course. It's surprised you'd be if you knew how

52

many people I'd 'dropped' over the years to prepare for just such an eventuality as this!"

"But what are you *doing* here? Are you still in the same business?"

"In the same *line* of business, boy; but by no means in the same way of business. That sweet little setup I had in Casablanca was the result of thirty years' hard work. You can't replace that overnight. But, thank the dear Lord, I still had me overseas contacts and there were one or two souls were prepared to lend me a quid or two till I was on me feet again—if you see what I mean —so it begins, it begins."

"In that case," Illya said, "maybe you could be of help again."

"But of course, of course. Always ready to oblige an old client. Here, you're still standing up! Sit you down, sit you down. Let me fetch you a little something to refresh yourself. A vodka?"

"I'd rather have a Steinhaegger with a nice cold beer as a chaser, if your cellar can run to that."

"Certainly." The fat man detached a small, square box, louvered on one side, from the arm of his chair, raised it to his mouth, pressed a button, and called, "Joana! Are you there?"

Kuryakin smiled. The device, which would bleep until whoever was carrying its mate answered, was the same pattern as those used for local communications by the operatives of U.N.C.L.E.

"Yes, sir. You wanted something?" The soft voice came from the transceiver in the Irishman's hand.

"I did. A Steinhaegger and *pils* for my guest; the usual for myself, if you please, my dear."

Again Illya grinned. "The usual," he said. "Still Turkish coffee and Izarra, is it?"

"Ah, yes. If you have the sweet tooth, it doesn't lessen as you get older. . . . Now, how can my poor embryo organization help you?"

The agent pulled a chair out from a delicately wrought white iron table, swung one leg over the seat, and sat down with his forearms folded over its back. "Well, now," he said, "it's like this . . ."

Twenty minutes later, after the voluptuous eighteen-year old with the flashing eyes had brought their second round of refreshments, O'Rourke leaned back in his chair and sighed.

"So what you feel might be useful," he said, "is a bit of a rundown on any set of circumstances that might link together the few facts you have and the disappearance of Mr. Williams?"

"That's about it, yes."

"The car accident, the murders, the death of the old man followed immediately by the departure of your friend for Brasilia, the cabled references to rivers and dams, the visit here to the public works bureau—plus, of course, the pretense that the women belonged to this comic missionary body," the Irishman said, ticking the items off on his fingers one by one. "Seven positive items to balance one negative: the absence of news from your friend." He drained his coffee cup, took the liqueur glass still half full of the acid-yellow Basque digestive in one hand, and wheeled himself away towards the apartment with the other.

"Make yourself at home," he said over his shoulder, "and we shall see what we can do. Though it's a case, mind, where I wish we had the use of a computer!"

Illya gulped down his *schnapps* and sipped the cold beer, relaxing in his chair as the drowsy sounds of afternoon washed over him. Bees probed the trumpets of petunia and busied themselves over the geraniums. An electric blue dragonfly darted under the vines, hovered for a moment in the shade, and then flashed away again into the sun. Across distant roofs the sounds of traffic rumbled.

From where he sat, he could see through a window into a room that seemed to be O'Rourke's office and workroom. There were gray steel filing cabinets along one wall, bounded at one side by the dials and pilot lights of a powerful transmitter, and on the other by two complex tape units with vertically mounted spools and a twelve-channel console. There was nothing to rival the comprehensive anarchy of the Irishman's old headquarters in Casablanca, but there were several tables covered in a chaos of magazines and newspapers and cuttings—all of them, Illya guessed, ringed and under-lined and coded and annotated in his own private and multi-colored system of cross-indexing. From time to time the man in the wheelchair himself was visible, cross-ing and recrossing the window, searching among piles of paper for pencils or notes, burrowing for the telephone. Once a tall, slim man with a heavy moustache, whom Illya thought he had seen once before, at the airport, came in and talked earnestly for some minutes.

And finally O'Rourke returned, the wheelchair spin-ning expertly to a halt beside the table, with his hands full of cuttings.

"You're in luck," he said. "I think we can help you . . . but first I have to ask—you know, the embarrassing bit! I have to—"

"Payment in advance, of course," Kuryakin said, reach-ing for his wallet. "Business as usual, in fact! What's the price?"

"Well now, you may recall that in the other place—we mention no names at all, in case there is any odium attaching to our former life!—in the other place there was the subscription system, for military attachés and the like continually wanting snippets of information and gossip about their rivals and so on and so forth?"

"Yes, I remember."

"And then there was the straight transaction—for ev-ery major piece of information obtained according to con-tract, one thousand dollars."

"Yes. I remember that even better."

"Just so. Well, here, I'm happy to say, the price is less—both because I'm only starting and you can't charge big league prices in the provincial games, and also be-cause I have so far got lower overheads."

"Excellent. What is the new price—nine hundred and ninety-nine?"

"You should never joke about money, Mr. Kuryakin," O'Rourke said reproachfully. "It is the one commodity we can never do without. The price is five hundred dol-lars."

"Plus twenty-five percent service charge?"

"Plus fifteen per cent. Here, I have less staff—and my service charge was just that: it all went to staff."

"Fine. Any state tax here—for protection, I think it was?"

"Ten percent only."

"Ten percent! It was *one* percent in—you know where."

"Sure, this is a modern country. You have to pay for advances in techniques."

"In all truth, the additional charges seem to come to within one percent of what they were before—however you split them up and whatever you call them!"

"On a sum only half the total to begin with, Mr. Kuryakin; on the smaller sum."

Illya shrugged ruefully and peeled off six hundred-dollar bills from his roll. He opened his wallet and added two tens and a five. "There you are, you old rogue," he said. "Now give!"

"The fee buys you to the right to the invective," the Irishman said placidly, folding the money and stuffing it into the breast pocket of his shirt. "And anyway, we've come up with something right away."

"And that is?"

"Dams, me boy. Dams. There are not but two in construction at the moment for which you could use Brasilia as a jumping-off point: one at Guadalara and the other at a place called San Felipe do Caiapo. And the first of these is a government project, all public observation platforms and conducted tours and I don't know what-all. So I doubt not 'tis the other we're after."

"And where is this other?"

"San Felipe? In the hills—and bare and barren they are, too!—behind the new city of Getuliana that they're after building. 'Tis a private enterprise, this, that some hook of a European talked the government into okaying, and the whole shoot comes under a small holding company run by a contractor named Moraes."

"You mean that all the subcontractors working on the dam are really tied up with this man's firm?"

"And those building the city, too. The whole blessed shoot!"

"That should be something for a monopolies commission to see!"

"It should that. But that's not all. Wait'll I tell you, boy: you remember telling *me* about that organization when I was in the other place . . . the boyos that blew up me dump and had me runnin'?"

"You mean Thrush?"

"I do. You recall you told me this was an international conspiracy of financiers, scientists, industrialists and political extremists who had only one aim—to rule the world?"

"I do."

"And you remember you said that Thrush had no allies, only enemies; that it might play off east against west or vice versa, but that it would never ally itself with either?"

"Yes."

"And that, in furtherance of its aims, it could draw on the latest electronic and other scientific aids—whole armies and air forces if necessary? And furthermore that it concentrated on infiltrating into every country by means of taking control of existing organizations?"

"Yes."

"And that when this was done, the organization continued to fulfill its ostensible role, though in fact below the surface it was dedicated to further the aims of Thrush?"

"Yes."

"And that organizations so perverted were termed 'satraps' and came under the control of Thrush's Central Council and the Ultimate Computer they use for policy-making?"

"Yes, yes—but I don't quite—"

"Well, then," the Irishman said, pausing for breath at last and sitting back in his wheelchair, "what would you say if I was to tell you that there had been a considerable interest in Thrush in my office ever since they put me out of business over there . . . and that I had *made* it my business to keep tabs on those boyos from time to time?"

"I should say it was very natural."

"You would, eh? Then you would not find it excessively unlikely that I'd know a bit more than the next man if those gentlemen were involved in anything?"

"No, I suppose not."

"Good. For I can tell you, Mr. Kuryakin, beyond any doubt, that there are twenty-eight sub-contractors employed on the construction of the San Felipe dam and the city of Getuliana—all hired through Moraes and his company. *And every single one of 'em is a Thrush satrap!*"

Illya whistled softly. "I see!" he said. "That does put a different complexion on the inquiry—and lend an air of urgency, too."

"It does that. And I can tell you some other things, too. First, that the so-called D.A.M.E.S. has been hired by a consortium of these firms to assist with resettling peasants dispossessed by the dam; second, that their behavior in the up-state region has caused a lot of comment; third, that the city of Getuliana is far behind schedule in building—the locals say it is only a blind to cover the unscrupulous lining of pockets, but more informed gossip considers it a blind for something else. . . . And the last point is just a name: Wassermann."

"Wassermann?"

"Yes. A European financier who has settled here with great success. In economic circles here and in Sao Paulo, one talks, in money matters, of the Wassermann Test: if a given amount of capital has doubled itself within two years—then two to one it's a Wassermann project!"

"I see. What he has got to do with this dam, then?"

"He chiseled the concession to build the city and the dam from the government. The whole deal lies within his giving, as it were. And he gave it all to Moraes. That's all."

"No hard and fast news of my Mr. Williams?"

"He asked questions in Brasilia. He asked questions in Goiás. He hired a car. It was returned—not by him. That's all."

"And the old man?"

O'Rourke spread his huge hands. "Who knows? They say there are an unusual number of American undesirables in the country, particularly *up*-country. And that these are balanced by bad men from other places. You can draw your own conclusions. . . . Now, let me write you a few notes with names, addresses and telephone numbers that you can memorize, and that will be all."

He pulled a small pad from an inside pocket and began scribbling on the topmost page. After half a minute, a thin, insistent piping sounded at the side of his chair.

He unhooked the tiny two-way radio and held it to his ear. "Yes," he said curtly. "What is it? . . . . No, I'm busy at the moment—Oh. Yes. Yes, perhaps you'd better come in, Raoul. We're on the terrace."

As he finished writing and handed the sheets to Illya, the tall moustached man that the agent had seen in the office walked onto the roof garden.

"You'd better tell Mr. Kuryakin what you told me," O'Rourke said. "Raoul here keeps a watch on arrivals and departures at the airport and generally has a finger on the pulse, you know."

The tall man bowed and spoke directly to Illya. "The senhor may not know it, but he has been followed ever since he left the New York plane," he said softly in Spanish-accented Portuguese. "The watcher booked into the same hotel, parked opposite the police headquarters when you were there, followed you to the district office and tailed you back to the car rental place, busied herself with a water-oil-tire checkup during the time you spent inside, was three behind you in the queue at the library, and finally followed you on foot until you encountered the boss here."

"Busied *herself*," Illya said faintly. "You did mean that the tail was feminine?"

"But yes. The senhor can see for himself." Raoul strode to the edge of the terrace and parted the vines. "See—by the bookshop window on the other side of the court, occupying herself with the bin of secondhand volumes: a very beautiful young lady with dark hair. . . ."

Chapter 6

A Lady Is Unmasked

BY THE TIME Illya had memorized the contents of the sheets given to him by O'Rourke and had taken his leave, it was almost dusk. The obvious thing to do now was to follow Solo to Brasilia as quickly as possible and try to pick up his trail near the dam. He went accordingly to the airline offices to inquire about planes.

And with him went the girl. Now that he knew he was being followed, the Russian watched her technique with interest—and it acted in some small way as a salve to his wounded professional pride to see how expert she was. She never hurried, she never dawdled, she never did anything obvious like staying too long at the wrong shop window, and yet she was always there; she was never close enough to notice, yet she was never too far behind to catch up and follow an unexpected move; she anticipated intelligently, after being already on the far side of the road before he had himself crossed; she varied her distance skillfully, and she made such masterful use of other people as cover that Kuryakin found it difficult to keep his eye on her for long enough to form an impression of her looks. Since he was determined that she should not realize he knew of her existence, he contented himself with occasional sideways glances at shop windows and occasional reflections from a cupped hand over a lens of his sunglasses. From what he could see, the girl was slender, about his own height, with a lean jawline and chiseled features thrown into dramatic relief by long dark hair drawn severely back by a crimson bandeau. Her suit was in some lightweight navy material with white revers, and she carried slung from one shoulder, unfashionably, a big white handbag on a strap.

To his surprise, the airline offices were shut. And so, he saw as he looked around, were the neighboring stores and offices.

"Excuse me," he said, stopping a passerby, "do you

know if these shops—the airline office in particular—will be open again later?"

White teeth flashed in a dark face. "Open later?" a deep voice chuckled. "Tonight? Man, you must be jokin'!"

"But I thought . . . Usually they're open until . . ."

"Usually is other days. You must be out of your mind! Don't you know what day it is?" the man said, passing on with a wave of his hand.

Illya saw a modern hotel across the road and went into the foyer. There seemed to be an extraordinary number of laughing, chattering people about in noisy groups. Some of the women were wearing paper hats.

"Excuse me," he said to the reception clerk. "I wonder if you could possibly find out for me whether there is a plane tonight—"

"*Tonight!*" the clerk exploded. He reached under his counter and came up with a half full bottle of champagne. "Tonight is not for planes, senhor," he caroled. "Have a drink. Be my guest—tomorrow we can think about airplanes." Strident giggling cut short his harangue and a group of teenage girls with linked arms infiltrated his cubbyhole to carry him away shouting and waving his bottle. Illya shrugged his shoulders and went out again. From behind him a burst of laughter and the sound of breaking glass were cut short by the closing of the swinging doors.

In the streets, now that he noticed it, there was an air of subdued excitement, a purpose and a direction to the knots of people hurrying all the same way. And there was a noise—distant, imprecise and exciting—that he suddenly realized he had been aware of deep in his subconscious for some time.

It was a composite, even a complex, sound . . . rising, falling, altering in pitch, almost hammering away at the threshold of hearing. And gradually, bit by bit, he came to separate the various components: there were voices, many many voices; there was the faint sound of musical instruments; there was clapping, cheering, shouting, laughing; there was the sound of multitudes of feet—and over and above everything there was a persistent muttering and thumping of hundreds of drums.

Almost against his will, Illya found himself carried along with the main body of the crowd. Darkness was thickening and strange illuminations flared over the rooftops to the east. Here was an opportunity to lose the tail if he wished to. Should he do so—or should he deliberately encourage the girl to keep in touch so that he could turn the situation to his own advantage later? He decided to let her stick. He wanted to find out exactly why she was following him and on behalf of whom. . . .

Now suddenly the road erupted into an open space on the far side of which stretched Copacabana Beach.

Kuryakin halted, amazed at the astonishing sight which met his eyes. The place was jam-packed with people, weaving and dancing and bouncing to the disparate music of at least a dozen different bands—guitars, mandolinas, accordions, flutes, an occasional trumpet or trombone, and everywhere the insistent pounding of percussion. There were hand-hit conga drums, timbales thrashed with flat sticks, tomtoms, snare drums, maraccas, claves, guiros and, above all, bongos beaten in a complexity of rhythms so intoxicating as to be irresistible. Into the surging mass of dancers flooding the spaces between the bands, a parade with huge *papier-mâché* masks, banners, and bobbing balloons in the shape of vast and grotesque beasts was forging its way, spearheaded by its own group of buglers. Great monsters in bright crêpe paper and wood floated in the air on wires, surrounded by clusters of more ordinary balloons and lines of ornate lanterns. Beyond, the enormous beach was black with people against the lines of phosphorescence rolled shorewards by the incoming tide.

As he watched, the sky was split by jots of fireworks fountaining into the dark from further along the promenade. A cheer burst from the celebrating throng and the dancing redoubled in energy.

It was, of course, Illya remembered, the season of *Carnaval*—and in Rio, Carnaval is something more than a religion! No wonder the man he had asked about the shops opening had been surprised.

More than half of the people in the colorful crowd were either garlanded or in some kind of costume, and around the square stalls and booths were selling streamers, paper hats and masks.

He turned—just in time to see, out of the corner of his eye, that the girl following him was buying a mask at a corner stall. It was a tall thing—a beaked animal rather like a North American Indian totem pole, with huge round eyes—and the wearer's own viewpoint was a slit halfway up the neck lost among a cascade of paper feathers falling almost to the ground.

Very well, the Russian thought with an inward smile. *Carnaval disguise is a game with room for more than one player....*

He turned aside and selected a giant head for himself, an outsized turnip shape with the orientally bucolic features of a Chinese coolie, surmounted by the three tiers of pagoda-shaped hats. From within the hollow sphere of this mask, he surveyed the merrymakers, who now stretched as far as he could see in either direction along the promenade. It would be a nice exercise in subtlety to swing the rôles around so that it was really he who was following the girl . . . by making sure that *she* followed *him* in the manner—and the direction—he wanted.

The density of the crowd made it harder to execute than to plan, however. He was continually caught up and hurried along in tidal waves of merriment—and when this happened, it was almost impossible to regulate his pace so that the girl was sure to be able to keep up. Nor was he able, so far, to burst out of the crowd altogether.

Struggling to beat his way against the tide, he caught isolated snatches of conversation as groups of people were carried past.

"Watcha say, boy! Slake it a while from this one, man . . ."

"Fabulous, just fabulous . . ."

". . . ever been kissed by a man with a beard before?"

"Hey, Charlie! Over here, Charlie . . . Hey, Charlie!"

". . . so colorful, I just can't *bear* it. Oh, *look* . . ."

"You got room for one more on that arm, handsome?"

"The drums go dudder-dudder bidder-bodder beeden-

63

dooden dadda—the same rhythm all the time—had you noticed?"

"... so beautiful, so lovely. I should like to ..."

"*Charleee!* ..."

The mask with the bird's beak and the paper feathers bobbed now near, now further away. Several times Illya was in danger of becoming separated from his follower by phalanxes of laughing, singing dancers with linked arms. Once he did lose sight of it altogether when an unexpected display of frenzied acrobatics from a girl in a tight blue dress attracted a howling circle of admirers between them. Then he caught sight of the mask again, further to the left than he had expected, and plunged in pursuit.

He strove, without making it obvious, to place himself in a position from which the girl could discreetly take up the chase again—for she must have lost him as much as he had lost her. But she had apparently given up, for he realized now that she was trying to reach the fringes of the crowd.

Try as he would, he could not overtake her and put himself in view—there was always some segment of the noisy throng which obtruded just as he was getting near. ...

They had drifted away from the sea front now and were pushing their way up a narrow street towards one of the heights which lay behind the old town. On all sides the throbbing of the combos, the rattle of tambourines and the yowl of electric guitars filled the air. The roadway was filled with a stream of *papier-mâché* mandarins, Popeyes and mythical beasts, all pressing down towards the sea. But the population here was predominantly colored, the laughter more boisterous, the dancing less inhibited.

Kuryakin followed the beaked mask as it threaded its way to the top of the street, across a cobbled square, and up a steep, stepped path traversing the side of a bluff sprinkled with wooden shacks among the trees. Several times the grotesque headed turned in a questing way—almost as though she knew that she was being followed and wanted to make sure he was still there, the agent thought with a frown.

He quickened his pace as the girl in the Carnaval mask sprang agilely across a gap in a ruined wall and began to climb a street—it was more of a path, really—so steep that it had to be buttressed every two yards with risers of planking pegged into the hard earth.

Again the beak swung his way as he closed the gap between them. The shanties clinging to the sides of the cliff were ablaze with light and shaking with music. This was getting ridiculous—he must approach her right away. Now . . .

As he panted up the steps, his eyes came level with the girl's hurrying heels. How odd, he thought, that she should be wearing rope-soled espadrilles with a smart town suit. Suddenly suspicious, he sped up, drew level with her—and halted. The girl in the mask had stopped outside the door of one of the huts. A dim light burned behind a window looking onto a tiny porch.

"Now just a minute . . ." Illya began, when the girl turned toward him, raised a pair of slender arms, and lifted the beaked mask from her head and shoulders.

"Man, I thought you was *never* going to catch up," she said with a silvery laugh. "Still, I guess it saves us walkin' all the way up here to get a drink, eh? And it *is* Carnaval time. . . ."

The Russian stood rooted to the spot. Above the girl's plump cheeks, lustrous violet eyes twinkled in an eighteen-year-old face the color of mahogany.

He was still cursing himself for not realizing that the vendors of Carnaval masks would sell many of the same type in one evening when he got back to his hotel—footsore and still a little humiliated at the embarrassing explanation he had had to make to the girl on the heights. All in all, it had not exactly been his day: when he hadn't realized it, he had been tailed; when he had wanted to be tailed, he had lost the follower; except for the good fortune of finding O'Rourke, all his inquiries had drawn blanks; and now he had made a fool of himself! . . . Better to write the whole day off, have a nice refreshing bath, and get up early to catch the first available plane to Brasilia tomorrow!

He unlocked his door, switched on the lights in his room and checked his personal "signposts" to make sure it had not been searched in his absence.

Dropping the ridiculous coolie's head on a settee, he dragged off his jacket and strode through to the bathroom to switch on the taps.

"This absurdly large perforated thing is a silencer," the girl said. She was sitting on the edge of the tub. "The gun behind it is small. It's a Berretta, and unless you shoot terribly accurately, you haven't a hope in hell of stopping a man with one. The only thing is—I'm afraid I do shoot terribly accurately."

She rose swiftly to her feet. "Now—into the other room, if you please," she said briskly. "There are one or two questions I want to ask you...."

Chapter 7

Trespassers Will Be Liquidated

ILLYA KURYAKIN slumped into an easy chair, sighed, and broke open a pack of cigarettes. "Look, I don't know who you are ..." he began.

"Put that down," the girl rapped. "I've seen that one before: the first cigarette to come out of that pack is a bolt of metal, painted white. It comes out fast, because there is a powerful spring inside the pack—and it hits me right between the eyes. By the time I've recovered consciousness, you have the gun."

The agent shrugged and tossed the pack onto the bed. There were unusual glints of copper in the mass of dark hair, he saw in the bright lights of the hotel room, and the face was even more rakish and thoroughbred than he had thought.

"All right," the girl was saying, "we'll have your hands lying along the arms of the chair if you please ... that's it ... and now perhaps you'll tell me just exactly who you are and what you're doing here."

"Surely we have the rôles reversed?" Kuryakin murmured. "Those are *my* lines you are saying."

The girl tossed her head impatiently. "I lose my temper easily," she warned, "and a slug from a Berretta can be very painful—through the ear or a wrist, for example."

"Oh, come now," the Russian said easily, leaning forward to rise from the chair. "You know very well you wouldn't use that thing, even if it is silenced."

He dropped abruptly back into his seat. He had seen the almost imperceptible whitening of the knuckle as the girl put the first pressure on the trigger. "So-ho," he said softly. "We really would have used it, would we? Or else we know enough to bluff—knowing also that a professional couldn't afford to take a chance on it."

"All right, all right," the girl said. "So you read the sign, which told me what *I* wanted to know too; so let's just assume we're both professionals, shall we, and go on from there? . . . I repeat: Who are you and what are you doing here?"

"My dear young lady, there is no secret about that: you could have found out simply by coming up to me and asking. There was no need for all the melodrama."

"I'm waiting."

"My name is Illya Kuryakin; I live in New York; and I am in Rio looking for a friend who has disappeared."

"What was his name and what was he doing here?"

"His name *is* Williams, I hope. He was investigating something for some friends of mine."

"Investigating what?"

"I'm sorry, but I do not think that is any of your business."

"That's just where you're wrong," the girl said. "It is just that which makes it my business. For these friends of yours on whose behalf the so-called Mr. Williams was investigating are actually friends of *mine*—and they have never heard of Mr. Williams!"

"Friends of yours?" the Russian echoed. "You're working for the D.A.M.E.S.? But this is ridiculous!"

"I did not say I was working for the Daughters of America Missionary Emergency Service. Your Mr. Williams affected to be doing that: he went all over, asking questions and searching around, claiming to be a lawyer briefed by the organization. This was not true; nor is there a New York lawyer named Williams with his particular description. Naturally enough, therefore, there are a number of interested parties wanting to find out what gives."

"I see. And you represent which one of them?"

"So, to begin with," the girl said, ignoring his questions, "I ask you once more: Who sent you here? And who sent Williams?"

"The same people."

"Thank you very much. And there's no use pretending to be a member of the C.I.A., the Brazilian counter-intelligence service, or any special branch of the Rio police. I have friends in many places and I have checked them all."

"I wouldn't presume," Kuryakin said. "I wasn't aware that this matter impinged in any way on espionage. . . . Look, a man has disappeared. I'm trying to find him. That's all."

"Are you working for any American organization?"

"No."

"Any Brazilian organization?"

"No."

"Any underworld group? Any international organization?"

"I told you. I'm hired. To find a man. The hirers are clients and their identity is privileged information. You know that."

"I'm not a policewomen. I have a gun on you. I don't have to observe the niceties of legal protocol. . . . You're a private detective?"

Illya glanced over the girl's shoulder and raised an eyebrow. "All right, Petersen," he said. "Don't hurt her —just take the gun."

The weapon remained steady as the girl said evenly, "The French windows are locked. The catch makes quite a noise when it is operated. The balcony is nine floors up. There is no drainpipe, no fire escape connecting with it, and no way of reaching it from the neighboring rooms. . . . Do you think I'd sit here with my back to the windows if I hadn't checked all this, for God's sake? I thought we agreed to consider each other professionals."

"My apologies for underestimating both your training and your intelligence," Illya said dryly. "What is your name?"

"Coralie Simone, if it matters. Don't you ever smile?"

"Only when something amuses me. Don't you?"

"I'm too busy to notice. Now . . . once more: Who hired you?"

"An organization calling itself Thrush," the agent said blandly.

"I never heard of it. What's that?"

"A syndicate of powerful and ruthless men dedicated to the overthrow of all legal government and the eventual despotism of the world."

"I don't believe you."

"Don't believe what—that there is such an organization, or that I am hired by it?"

"I don't believe either of them."

"Well, I've heard of candor," Kuryakin said, "but this really is something. . . ."

Although the affair of the windows had not fooled the girl into turning around—he hadn't thought it would—the subsequent exchange had sufficiently diverted and held her attention for him to do what he wanted to. He was sitting fairly well forward in the chair, his forearms lying along its padded arms. The chair, he knew, ran very easily on its castors across the tiled floor. Imperceptibly, as he had talked and held her eyes with his own, he had drawn his feet back under him and edged his hands forward so that the fingers now dropped over the front ends of the chair arms. His center of gravity now should be such that, if the chair was suddenly removed from under him, he could stay in the same squatted position and not fall over. He flexed his muscles experimentally. . . . Yes. He could make it.

The time had come to end the interview. He wasn't sure at all that the girl was employed by the D.A.M.E.S. If she was, surely they would have liaised with Waverly. On the other hand, he couldn't believe she was a

Thrush member. Even the most accomplished of actresses could hardly have feigned that bland incredulity when he'd mentioned the organization and its aims. In any event, the riddle of her allegiance must wait until another time: at the moment, he was tired of being questioned himself.

". . . essential that you tell me your principals," Coralie Simone was saying.

Once more, Illya searched for, caught and held her eyes. "But surely you must realize, my dear . . ." he began.

Tensing the muscles of calf, back and thigh, he raised himself minutely from the chair and sent it rocketing backwards with a powerful thrust of his fingers.

The girl's eyes tore themselves away from his as the chair skated across the floor with a rumble and a screech. Involuntarily, she followed its path with her glance. At the same time, like a *trepak* dancer from the Cossack country, Kuryakin kicked out one leg horizontally from his squatting position.

The toe of his shoe caught the underneath of the gun's butt as it nestled in her hand, sending the weapon spinning upwards. Before she had switched her gaze back from the errant chair, he had risen to his feet, stretched out a hand and snatched the Berretta from the air.

"Forgive the liberty," he said quietly. "I have to leave early in the morning and I really do need some sleep."

The girl, scarlet with anger, her eyes flashing, nursed her hand and watched as he broke the automatic, slid the clip out and shook the shells into the palm of one hand. He crossed the room to the bed, picked up the white shoulder-strap bag she had left there, and dropped them inside. Then he bowed, handed her the bag and the empty gun, and turned to open the door for her. He was smiling.

"Until the next time, Miss Simone," he said gently.

"If there is one," the girl said grimly. "I do not like people opening my handbag without my permission. It's rude. Also, I have a rooted objection to being followed. So if you'll forgive me . . ."

She reversed the gun in her hand and slashed the butt

expertly down to the side of Illya's head while he was bent over the lock.

He still had a headache when the plane landed at Brasilia the following morning. The weather was humid, close and fiercely hot, the sky overcast by a lowering front.

In view of O'Rourke's information, he decided to go first of all to the auto rental companies. It wasn't until the fourth attempt that he found anyone who had heard of "Mr. Williams." But the boy behind the shabby counter in this one remembered at once.

"Why goodness me, yes!" he exclaimed, his dark face lighting up at the memory. "As a matter of fact he hired the car personally from me. Nice chap, really top-hole."

"He was going up to the San Felipe dam, was he?"

"Oh rather. Absolutely. Told me so himself, don't you know. In fact he asked me to help him work out the jolly old route. He was going to spend the night at Goiás, I believe."

"He didn't bring the car back himself?"

"Well, no. As a matter of fact a different bloke did. Just handed it in, paid out the cash and hooked it, you know."

"And you haven't seen Mr. Williams since?"

"Williams? No. Not a hide nor a jolly old hair. But . . ."

"You have seen the other man?"

"Not to say since, old bean. Before. I've seen him around. Cove by the name of Greerson. Hardly the type I'd expect your friend—"

"Does he live here?"

"Live here? Who *does*, old chap, who *does*? No, I fancy he's a backwoodsman. Tell you the truth, I rather thought he was a foreigner employed on the construction site or something of that sort."

"You've been very helpful," Illya said. "Here, take this —and I'd like to rent a car myself for a few days. Any chance at all of getting the same one Williams had?"

"Oh, I say, thanks awfully. Most decent of you. . . . Not to say the same actual one. One just like it—another

VW. But you can't very well have the actual one—the girl's already taken that."

"The girl?"

"Smashing bird, old boy. About an hour ago. Asked all the same questions you've asked—and off she drove."

Kuryakin gave an exclamation of annoyance. If the girl was Coralie Simone, it meant she had help in a big way. For she hadn't been on the first plane, he could have sworn—and that in turn meant she must have a private aircraft, for to have made Brasilia from Rio in any other way would have been impossible in the time.

"Don't you find that collar uncomfortable in this weather?" he asked sourly as they turned together to go out into the garage.

San Felipe do Caiapo was a collection of shacks, some wood, some adobe-and-thatch, dispersed around a rutted open space that did service as central square, market, sports ground and local park. There was an inn, a mud walled church, a swaying bridge over the river, and a garage—an open shed flanked by a single rusty gasoline pump which was surrounded by an assortment of decrepit vehicles. Without exception, these were of pre-war vintage and looked as though they had just managed to struggle as far as San Felipe when they were new, and had never been able to raise the necessary horsepower to leave again.

Most of the population were seated outside the front doors of their houses, leaning against the walls to get the maximum amount of shade from the projecting eaves, but there were several groups of men along a boardwalk linking the building on one side of the square rather in the manner of a Hollywood western.

Illya bumped the Volkswagen across the *plaza*, scattering chickens, dogs and mules, and edged the car cautiously over the bridge. There was only a trickle of water in the pebbly river bed below.

Beyond the town, the road twisted through a belt of forest, breasted a rise, and dropped down to the river again, where it joined a wider, paved highway running almost due north and south. Kuryakin took the northerly direction and headed for Getuliana. Presently the valley widened, the hills at each side became lower, and the river looped away in a series of ox-bows across an alluvial plain.

In a few miles, he caught sight of the new city. Or, rather, the place where the new city was destined to be.

The road clung to higher ground at the side of the wide valley, and the excavations—a couple of miles away in the middle of the plain—were spread out before him like a map. Hundreds of acres had been cleared, bulldozed into squares and rectangles and crescents, segmented by radial boulevards converging on a central space, laterally divided by wide avenues. But apart from the temporary huts erected by contractors, there wasn't a building in sight. A cloud of dust above the yellowish earth marked the place where a single bulldozer was working near a pair of cranes in one corner of the vast site. But the only other activity Illya could see was a mile away to the north, where the antlike movements of a fleet of trucks and several dozen men centered on a pair of heavy-bellied transport aircraft drawn up at one end of a wide landing strip.

Soon the distant puttering of the bulldozer was submerged in a heavier, deeper rumble. For a moment, he sought the source of the noise. Then his eye caught a moving dust cloud to his right. A column of trucks was winding its way along a route leading from the site to the road he was on. In a few minutes, the convoy roared past, heading for San Felipe and the dam. All the trucks were covered—and each one seemed to have a man in some sort of uniform beside the driver.

It was unbearably hot parked in the sunlight at the edge of the road. Making up his mind suddenly, Kuryakin swung over the VW's wheel and set off the way he had come, following the convoy back towards the dam.

Three or four miles after the junction with the road to San Felipe village, the valley narrowed and the sides became steep and rocky. Soon he was driving along a serpentine defile above whose thickly wooded lower slopes great cliffs reared skywards.

Abruptly, the gorge divided: the river in its stony bed

burrowed beneath the road and was seen to be emerging from the canyon on the right, while the tributary valley on the left was marked only by a dried-up watercourse showing not even a trickle of moisture. The road forked too, though in a contrary sense—for while the highway to the south twisted away towards the pass at the head of the minor valley, the road following the main gorge was blocked a hundred yards further on by wire mesh gates on steel frames. And the smooth blacktop which had distinguished the highway ever since Getuliana swerved aside from the main road and continued beyond the gates to where, a half mile away, the great bulk of the dam itself was visible around a bend in the valley. Beyond a cracked and peeling sign pointing to AGUACA-LINDA—SANTA MARIA DA CONCEICAO—GOIAS the trunk road relapsed at once into an unsurfaced dirt-track alternating chassis-breaking potholes with extrusions of naked bedrock. Clearly the pavement had been laid only to assist the contractors in moving materials from landing strip to dam, and the hell with local communications.

Illya had no means of knowing how wide the reservoir might be in the drowned valley behind the *barrage*, but the actual dam was one of the highest he had ever seen. From the curved lip spanning the gorge high up against the blue wedge of sky, the great curtain of concrete plunged downwards in three stages like a frozen wave. At each level, multiple arches housing the sluices linked blockhouses from which the giant-bore pipes dropped to the hydroelectric generating station below. And around the power station an ancillary web of transformer housings, masts, insulators and pylons had been neatly spun. Towering between the age-old rock faces of that desolate valley, the dam was a testament to the ingenuity of man, a beautiful piece of engineering.

The agent drove slowly up to the wire gates blocking the road to the power station. On either side as far as he could see, ten-foot wire fencing behind a deep ditch guarded the boundaries of the property. A man came out of a small concrete building just inside the gates. He was dressed in the same khaki and black uniform worn

74

by the guards Illya had seen in the convoy. And he was carrying a machine pistol.

"What do you want?" he called over the top of the gates. His voice was not friendly.

"This is the San Felipe dam, isn't it?" Illya called, putting his head out of the car window. "The Moraes-Wassermann project?"

The guard continued staring at him, saying nothing.

"I am a construction engineer . . . in Brazil on a short visit to survey progress in hydroelectric works, bridging, and so on. They tell me the *barrage* here is particularly interesting and I wondered—"

"This is private property," the man said. "On your way."

"Most dams are on private property, but that does not mean that a courteously worded request—"

"I said beat it," the guard snapped, his sullen face scowling. "We don't like snoopers around here. Like I said, it's private, see. Now get out."

"But how can I get to see the artificial lake . . ."

"You can't. You can either go back to San Felipe or go on to Aguacalinda or Goiás—if you like driving over bare rock. And you won't see the lake from either road, because it's not overlooked by any goddam road. It's too high up and the rocks are too steep around it. . . . There's a third choice: you stay here one minute more, I'll call out the site police and have you towed off our property. And they're not gentle."

"Well, really. . . . I'm not on your property anyway. I'm outside the gates."

"You're on private property the moment you leave that fork. Now are you getting the hell out of here, or . . ."

Hoping that he had displayed the correct amount of outraged resentment to pass for a visitor consumed merely with idle curiosity, Illya turned the Volkswagen and drove on towards Aguacalinda. Although the surface was very bad, the road appeared—judging from the multiplicity of tire marks in the dust—to carry fairly heavy traffic.

Such few houses that he saw, however—mainly peas-

75

ant huts or the dwellings of subsistence farmers who scratched a living from the stony soil—were strung out along the hillside far from the road without even a track wide enough for a vehicle leading to them. So the traffic must either be heading all the way south to Goiás and the next state (which seemed unlikely) or to some other place further up the valley. Yet the maps he had, admittedly imprecise, showed no sign of any large-scale habitation before Aguacalinda . . . which was some distance on the other side of the pass and was in any case smaller than San Felipe itself.

If the maps were in any way correct, the valley which had been drowned by the reservoir curved around and ran almost parallel with the one he was in right up to the watershed. Between the trees to his right every now and then he could see the high wire fence enclosing the property—which seemed to confirm the geographers in their mapping.

When he was two or three miles from the gates and the guard house, he stopped the car under a grove of trees and climbed the steep side of the valley on the opposite side of the road from the fence.

The trees were dense and for the first half hour it was tough going. Then he came out onto a stretch of rocky ground where it was easier to pick his way. And finally he stopped where the rough slope met the vertical cliffs lining the gorge.

But the guard had been right. Even from here he could see nothing of the artificial lake beyond the far side of the defile. Behind the opposite rock face the barren ground rose again and cut off his view before it dropped to the next valley. At his feet, the road and the dried up river bed snaked through the trees.

He scrambled back down the mountainside and crossed the road to examine the wire fence.

As he had expected, there were alarm wires threaded along its length—although these were surprisingly not electric, but the simple mechanical kind which actuated buzzers or bells. Every few yards there were notices saying: DANGER! THIS IS PRIVATE PROPERTY. KEEP OFF! WARNING IS GIVEN TO TRESPASSERS THAT THE GROUND BE-

He returned to the car and drove on. After another mile and a half, the fence curved away up the steepening hillside to pass around a sizable property bordering the road. There was a long, low, two-storied house with wooden balconies, a group of outbuildings, and palm trees behind a high hedge of some shrub. An estancia, would it be? A hacienda? . . . No, that was Spanish, surely. But anyway it was a demesne very different in style from the poor cabins scattered along the other side of the valley.

It was when he had gone about ten minutes' drive past the place, and the road was beginning to zigzag upwards, obviously on its way to the saddle across the watershed, that he realized the evidence of heavy traffic was no longer visible. The dusty spaces between the potholes were bare of tire marks.

He turned and drove back towards the property, pulling the VW off the road a quarter of a mile short of it and running the car behind a thicket to hide it from the road.

Once again he forced his way up the hillside to the rock face and scanned the valley below through field glasses.

The estancia was clearly visible beyond a stretch of woods. Behind the dense hedges, there seemed to be quite a number of people busied about various tasks, among them a number of women in the distinctive green tweed uniforms of the D.A.M.E.S. *They must be sweltering in those clothes at this temperature!* Illya thought.

There were several station wagons and a few private cars parked between the house and the barns. As he watched, some large American convertible carrying three men and three girls prowled around the edge of the building and cruised down towards the gate. One of the girls got out to open the gate and then the car sped away northwards towards Getuliana in a cloud of dust. Judging from their movements, all six of the occupants appeared to be somewhat drunk.

Illya's binoculars had remained trained on the gateway, though. The powerful Zeiss lenses clearly showed up the beaten earth of the entrance—and the myriad marks of heavy wheels passing over it. The mystery of where all the traffic on the road had gone was solved: obviously all of it turned in here!

But where did the heavy trucks go when they had made the turn? There were none visible there now—and although the estancia was large enough, there was certainly no accommodation for convoys as big as the one he had seen leaving the airstrip earlier. There had still been trucks loading material from the transport planes when he had left to follow the first convoy, however; even if he had lost the first one, there should be a second coming along some time soon. Then he could find out.

He would have to find a different viewpoint, nevertheless. Various belts of trees intercepted his vision where he was now. He began working his way back down towards the car.

When he was about halfway there, he emerged from a screen of bushes to find a poorly dressed Indian standing with his back to him on a piece of level ground, staring flint-faced across the valley at the estancia.

"Nice place?" Kuryakin said, lacking a suitable opening.

The Indian swung slowly around and stared at him impassively.

"I mean, it's a bit of a surprise, finding a big place like that out here," Illya went on. "All the others are so small, you know."

"Nice place, sure, if you have money," the Indian said bitterly.

"It belongs to rich people, then? From the city?"

"Surprise, too, to all the people live here. All the people have houses and farms that are take away and put under lake," said the man—who appeared to make a practice of answering always the question *before* the one that had just been asked.

The agent looked suitably encouraging and said nothing.

"I had a farm—small place, but I like—over there," the

78

Indian continued, waving an arm towards the opposite side of the valley. "Now it is take away and I am given small, poor house here with stony ground and some money. But money cannot give me back thirty years work on that farm—and my father before. Now I am not even allowed to walk past and look into water!"

"But I thought the ladies down there dressed in green had helped to iron out—or—to—to make easy all the problems with those who had to move for the dam."

"Ladies!" the man burst out. "Ladies? Our women are not allowed to behave like that in private—and certainly not in public. It is disgrace . . . drunken and singing and shouts and unseemly acts."

"Really? You surprise me. But this is an American—"

"Why should these foreign women be permitted to mock our customs in this way? It is disgrace."

"Understood. This is not the first time I have heard such complaints. Do *all* the women connected with the dam behave like that?"

But the Indian suddenly bit his lower lip, an expression of guarded watchfulness closing up his face. "I say too much," he muttered. "It is not permitted. It is forbidden to speak of these matters."

"By whom?"

"The gods will be angry and spoil our crops."

"Who says so? Who says you mustn't speak?"

"The caboclo. It is instruction."

"Caboclo?"

"The old one, the mouthpiece of the spirits. Paí Hernando told me so. Through the caboclo he speaks with the spirits."

"*What* name did you say?" Illya almost shouted.

"Paí Hernando. The father-of-saint at the Candomblé down there."

"That place is a Candomblé headquarters?"

"Not whole place. There is a Condomblé *tenda* behind."

"And the name of the—father-of-saint?—his name is Hernando and he speaks with the spirits through a guide, a caboclo?"

"Paí Hernando, yes."

Illya was whistling to himself as he ran down the remainder of the slope to the Volkswagen. He had felt all along that he was on the right scent. Now, surely, this *must* be the "Hernando's Hideaway" which had so puzzled them in Napoleon Solo's telegram. . . .

He put his key in the Volkswagen's lock and twisted. The key refused to turn.

Puzzled, he tried again. Again he could make no impression. He stood back and stared at the vehicle . . . and realized suddenly that it wasn't his own. It was the same color, the same model, the same year. But the registration number was one integer different—and inside, tossed carelessly onto the back seat, was the cockaded hat of a member of the D.A.M.E.S.

It must be the car hired by the girl, Coralie Simone—indeed, now that he had oriented himself, he could see the top of his own gleaming through the thicket a little way to the north.

And if this was Coralie Simone's car—and if the boy at the car rental company had told the truth—then this was the actual one Solo had been driving in this very area a few days ago. And Solo himself, alive or dead, must be somewhere on the other side of the wire fence beyond the place he had called Hernando's Hideaway. . . .

Chapter 8

A Break-In—And A Surprise!

ILLYA CAME upon the girl quite unexpectedly. He had decided to leave the car where it was and approach the estancia on foot, reasoning that the people in charge were less likely to notice a strange vehicle if it was further on up the valley, beyond their gates. He had been forced to cross the road to the side where the wire fence ran, because the river bed was immediately alongside the entrance road and there was no cover on the opposite side. And he had plunged deeper into the bushes between road and fence, first to avoid being seen by two tough-looking men and two overpainted girls in a red Jaguar which had roared past in the direction of the pass, and secondly when he had heard the second convoy arriving.

It was while he was watching the twelve two-tonners turn in at the gate of the estancia that he heard the girl's gasp of pain.

The sound seemed to come from only a few feet away, just on the far side of a clump of oleanders lining the ditch. Cautiously, he parted the branches with their scarlet flowers and peered through.

The fence was immediately beyond the ditch—and just behind it was the girl, her arm bent up behind her back by one of the uniformed men who obviously patrolled the whole perimeter around the dam. She was dressed in D.A.M.E.S. uniform now. Against the pallor of her cheeks, her hair shone richly in the sun.

"Come on, sweetheart," the guard was saying in English. "You know as well as I do that you're not allowed on this side of the fence. Now how'd you get over, and what are you doin', huh?"

"You're hurting my arm," the girl said. "*Oh* . . . I–I walked around from the gates. Down by the powerhouse."

"Don't give me that," the man rasped. "The gates are five miles from here and your shoes are still polished—there's not even a scratch on 'em!"

"I can't help that. . . . *Will* you let go of my arm—"

"You come across from the estancia that's what, ain't it? Now you know you birds got no business this side of the wire . . . that's why Macdonald would never let you through at the gates. Either you go through the mountain or you stay outside at the estancia, right? . . . Now I'm gonna take you right back to the guardroom and we'll see what . . ."

And suddenly he was on the ground. Illya could not see exactly how it was done—an ankle was placed to one side, a trim hip was thrust out and something expert took place with the arm that had been held up behind the girl's back—but the result was that the guard, momentarily inattentive as his thoughts ran ahead, found himself flying through the air over Coralie Simone's shoulder.

He landed flat on his back among the grasses. There were lumps of limestone hidden by the tussocks and the force of the impact would have knocked out many men. But this one was tough. He was on his feet almost at once, lips snarled back from discolored teeth, approaching the girl like a wrestler, with outstretched hands.

His mistake was to go on thinking, after the initial surprise, that he could handle the thing himself. Had he blown the whistle that hung around his neck on a chain, that would have been that: a patrol of men would have been down on them within minutes and the girl would have been taken prisoner. But with the arrogance of the true bully, the guard was confident that he could overpower a mere woman.

From behind his screen of oleanders, Kuryakin watched the man and the girl circling each other over the rough ground. He wasn't sure what to do. There was an overhanging branch from a big tree some way down the fence; he could probably swing himself across without disturbing the alarm wire there. Yet there was a risk that the guard might see or hear him on the way to it. And they had to avoid at all costs any attempt to summon help.

In the event, the decision was taken from the Russian's hands. Having had three attempts at grappling with his adversary frustrated by well timed judo grips, the guard began to lose his temper. He leaped at the girl with flailing fists.

Coralie Simone sprang agilely away towards the fence —but as she went, one heel caught in a projection of rock concealed among the grasses and she stumbled backwards. With a growl of triumph, the guard was on her, pinning her arms to her sides in a bear hug and forcing her to the ground. The girl brought one sharp knee up into his stomach as she tried desperately to free her arms. She twisted her head and sank her teeth into the rough material of his sleeve, attempting to bite through the cloth to the muscles of the biceps beneath. She jerked her forehead back and forth trying to butt him in the face.

The man chuckled and spun her around as easily as if her body had been a bale of cotton. As she lay face downwards in the tall grass, he kneeled on the backs of her thighs and seized the collar of her jacket in both hands. The green stuff ripped up the back seam as he yanked with all his strength and the garment came away from her in two pieces.

As he grunted in triumph and in amusement, his eyes looked through the wire strands of the fence and met the glittering stare of Kuryakin concealed among the leaves on the other side.

Before the round O of his mouth could utter the cry of astonishment it was framing, the agent's forefinger had tightened on the trigger of the miniature automatic in his hand. The weapon—it looked no more dangerous than a gadget cigarette lighter—emitted a staccato *chock!* and the guard keeled over backwards. As he crashed down among the grasses, the girl got shakily to her feet.

"You!" she said, seeing Kuryakin. "What are *you* doing here? . . . I suppose I ought to thank you, though I could have handled him perfectly well myself. Even so . . ." She looked dubiously down at the fallen guard.

"Do not worry," Illya said. "I dislike violence and I never kill unnecessarily. It was just what we call a sleep dart; he will be *hors de combat* for an hour, that's all. So far as thanks go, I think I deserve them . . . considering that I still have a headache from our last meeting."

Coralie Simone blushed. "I'm sorry about that," she said, "but I wanted to make sure you didn't follow me here."

"You could have saved yourself the trouble, as you see. Why not?"

"Because I have an investigation to carry out and I don't like snoopers. You wouldn't say who you were."

"So have I and neither would you. But before we start quarreling again let us deal with this man—otherwise both our investigations will fail." He rose to his feet, made his way to the tree with the overhanging branch and worked his way along it until he could drop safely to the ground on the far side of the fence.

"The sleep dart will take care of this specimen for an hour," he said as he came up to the girl and the recumbent guard. "But I need him to be out of the way for at least two—so that he cannot possibly raise an alarm until I'm well away. If only I knew how often he is supposed—"

"He patrols a five hundred yard sector of the fence," the girl said crisply. "I've been checking. He doesn't have to make contact—or not necessarily—with the men on either side. There is no overlapping. And he isn't due for relief for another three hours."

"So he's just possibly not going to be missed?"

"Exactly. We are more than a hundred and fifty yards from the nearest adjoining sector."

The agent was rolling the unconscious guard over onto his face. "Okay," he said. "So if we take off his belt . . . so . . . and strap his arms to his sides . . . like *this* . . . and lash his wrists together with his tie . . . we should be able to prolong his period of forced inactivity beyond the hour given to us by the dart. Now what about his knees, his ankles, and some sort of gag?"

"You could use this," the girl said doubtfully. "It's of no further use to me now." She was holding up the two torn halves of her jacket.

Kuryakin took the green tatters from her. He ripped a back panel into three sections, binding the guard's ankles with one, his knees with another, and using the third to tie into place a wadded handkerchief which he rammed into the man's open mouth. "That should keep him out of the way until they start to look for him when he doesn't report at the end of his shift," he murmured as they dragged the bound and gagged man into the shelter of a thorn bush. "Now what about you, young . . . Aha!"

"What is it, Sherlock Holmes?"

The agent was looking at the remaining half of the D.A.M.E.S. jacket which he held in his hands. Below the torn collar a name tape, shiny with continued use, slightly soiled from contact with other clothes, was neatly sewn. On the pale ribbon, red letters spelled out C. SIMONE.

"Unless your principals specialize in detail work more perfect than any used by the world's intelligence services," Illya said slowly, "this is an old jacket that's been worn a lot. It really is your own garment—not a cover disguise. You really do work for the D.A.M.E.S."

"Of course I do," the girl said impatiently. "I work for the Special Investigation section. Lots of our girls come from very particular families and we have to take special care about conditions and so on when we send teams abroad. We're always having to make inquiries about one thing or another—and of course when we find people pretending to be D.A.M.E.S. when they're not, then naturally the Committee wants to find out why."

"But why didn't you say so? It would have saved so much—"

"How like a man! Why should I tell you? Who are you, anyway?"

"I work for the United Network Command for Law and Enforcement. The man who is missing is a colleague of mine from the same Section."

"So you're from U.N.C.L.E.! Why didn't *you* tell *me*?"

"Because I didn't . . ." Illya sighed in exasperation. "Because nobody told me you would have a representative down here. I imagine they didn't know."

"No, they wouldn't," Coralie Simone said. "We didn't tell you."

"Why on Earth not?"

"Mrs. Stretford—the Commandant—said that since your Mr. Waverly couldn't be bothered to be cooperative, she didn't see why she should."

"So you wasted all that time checking on me, and I— Never mind! Since we are both trying to find out what's going on here, suppose we join forces for the time being, okay?" Illya smiled his rare and charming smile.

The girl hesitated. Then the smooth skin around her eyes crinkled delightfully, the wide mouth stretched in the lean face. There was a flash of teeth. "Agreed," she cried with a laugh. "It's a deal—for the time being!"

"Splendid. What now, then? I'm trying to find out what goes on in the grounds of that estancia back there."

"So am I. All the trucks seem to go there and not along the made-up road leading to the power station. I want to have a closer look. Do you think . . . if we kept on this side of the fence and circled the place from above . . ."

Kuryakin was shaking his head. "Not a chance," he said. "Even if we could make it past the guards and the dogs, there's not a shadow of cover. Look!" His gesture encompassed the sweep of bare hillside above the trees masking the estancia, the slant of rocky slope beyond it, and the barren wall of cliff rising behind that. "Do you have a change of clothing in the car?"

"Yes," Coralie said. "Why?"

"Because I'm going to make a frontal foray. As long as you are not dressed like one of their spurious D.A.M.E.S. you can be my assistant when I ask for information about the Candomblé."

"Candomblé. I keep hearing that word. I've spoken to a lot of the local Negroes, and some Indians too. All of them seem afraid to talk about the dam—even if they've been forced to leave their homes by the scheme —because of the Candomblé. What is it, a secret society?"

"Not exactly. More like a religion. There are a number of different cults here in Brazil—all of them a mixture of African and Indian worship with Christianity and Spiritualism. The two most affecting simple Negro and Indian people are Candomblé and Umbanda. In both cases, their gods are a mixture of Christian and pagan ones; both believe that you can communicate with those gods or their representatives by means of mediums. But the initiates of Candomblé—so it is believed—can be visited by, or get in touch with, their gods personally, whereas the *umbandistas'* mediums have to have the gods' wishes interpreted through a guide, rather in the manner of a western séance."

"How fascinating," the girl said. "But why the difference?"

"I don't know too much about it," Kuryakin replied. "But the main reasons go back to the days of slavery. The most intelligent African slaves brought over to

Brazil were the Yoruba. They had the most complex religions and gods—and the mixture of these with Catholicism produced Candomblé ... the cult with the strongest African influence, radiating outwards from Bahia. The less developed Bantu from Angola, centered more on Rio, were that much more swayed by the great Spiritualist movement which swept Brazil in the last century, and their cult is the one called Umbanda today."

"But why should a religious cult bar local people from—"

"We'll ask," Illya said, interrupting, "when we get there."

But the tall, white haired Negro with the Harvard accent and the lined face who met them in the Candomblé *tenda*—a wooden building like a mission hut which stood among trees to one side of the estancia—was uncooperative. They had not been challenged at the gate and they had followed the drive, which skirted the building and then sloped downhill towards a thicket, until a signpost had directed them towards the hut. A Negro woman in a white robe had left them in a waiting room while she'd gone to call Paí Hernando.

"If—as you claim—you are an anthropology graduate from the University of Southern California," the priest said in his well-modulated voice, "I cannot understand why you and your assistant should have chosen to come all the way here to this very modest, uninspiring *tenda* when there are so many others more interesting elsewhere." He sat at a simple desk. Through the uncurtained window behind him, they could see groups of men in the now familiar khaki and black uniforms moving among the trees.

"But that's just it," Illya said. "*All the way* here. Since Candomblé is centered on Bahia state and the areas to the north and east of it, we find it intensely interesting, demographically, to find a *tenda* as far west as this. We had no idea the Yoruba had ever been transported this far."

"They probably migrated after abolition. And in any case the boundary between former slave peoples and the

87

Indian aboriginals is hopelessly blurred now," Hernando said. He flicked a speck of dust from his pale gray suit and drummed his fingers on the top of the desk.

"As the priest in charge of this place," Coralie asked suddenly, "can you explain why the *spirits* should frown on the local people talking about this dam? We wondered how the forced moves had affected them, sociologically, but we couldn't get a soul to talk about it at all. They say the gods forbid."

"I am only Paí Hernando, the horse on which the spirits ride," the Negro said. "It is not for me to question the wisdom of the Orixás, the great ones. Indeed, I had no idea such messages had been transmitted through me. And now," he added pointedly, "if you could tell me how I can help you . . ."

"We should very much like to see some ceremonies—perhaps an *ôrunkó*—to compare with those performed in the Candomblés further east."

"I am afraid that is quite impossible. This is a simple country place. No such rituals take place here."

"But I thought . . ."

"Definitely not, sir. Apart from which, the local folk are—as you have seen—superstitious and suspicious. They would resent any outside participation, any hint of an *audience*, at their devotions."

Illya rose from his chair and paced up and down. "But surely," he cried agitatedly, running his hand through his pale hair, "there must be *something* in a cult which can impose so strong a taboo on the discussion—"

"I regret extremely," Paí Hernando said, rising to his feet also, "that I cannot help you at all. It is a pity that you should have traveled so far and so fruitlessly. Had you inquired first . . ."

"Are those soldiers out there?" Coralie asked innocently as he showed them to the door.

"Certainly not," the Negro said. "They are members of the construction company's security guard. There is valuable property in here."

"Your *tenda* is financed by the company, then?"

"By no means. They have been very generous, allowing us to operate on their land, granting us certain facilities."

"That aspect of paternalism in a foreign concern is interesting," Illya said. "Perhaps we could ask you a new—"

"Good day to you," Paí Hernando said firmly. He closed the door.

"Well, I've heard of visitors being discouraged," Coralie exclaimed as they walked out of the gates, "but this is ridiculous. Did you see those—security guards, did he say? I'm sure they'd have fired on us if we had turned right instead of left when we left that hut!"

"They probably would," the agent said soberly. "Obviously the entire Candomblé thing is a cheap device to blackmail the locals into silence about the whole project. The thing's a fake from beginning to end."

"Why are you so sure?"

"Several reasons. In the first place Paí Hernando, Father Hernando, is a form of address used in Umbanda associations, not in Candomblé. If there *is* a priest at a Candomblé *tenda*—and it's usually a priestess, as it happens—he would be called a Babalorixá, a Father-of-Saint. Caboclo, the term for an Indian guide, is from the Umbanda vocabulary too. . . . Second, to say they hold no ceremonies such as an *ôrunkó* is absurd: the *ôrunkó* is the be-all and end-all of Candomblé—the ceremony at which the initiates are 'visited' by their particular deities. And finally, if it was a genuine *tenda* it would have been surrounded by miniature huts—the dwelling places for particular gods, which have to be sited at particular spots. Did *you* see any shrines, any offerings, any *despachos* there?"

"No," the girl said. "I didn't see those twelve trucks anywhere either. Did you?"

The Russian smiled. "There were no trucks to be seen," he said. "But when I started my pacing-up-and-down routine, I was able to catch sight of a space behind those trees at the bottom of the slope. There's a cliff which comes right down to ground level there—a fault or something in the rock, so that there's no gradual slope there. But there is something else; I could see it quite clearly. The drive runs right up to the cliff—and then straight into it."

"Do you mean there's a tunnel?" Coralie gasped.

"A tunnel leading into the mountain, or through it. With a double row of lights in the roof and a concrete blockhouse at the entrance. So the mystery of the disappearing convoys is a mystery no more. They go on and through—and as soon as we have an opportunity to take them by surprise, that's what we have to do too."

"Yes, I see," the girl said thoughtfully. "That's what the guard meant, of course. 'Either you go through the mountain or you stay in the estancia'—that's what he said, isn't it?"

Kuryakin nodded. "They seem especially determined that nobody shall so much as glimpse the *surface* of this marvelous lake," he mused. "It seems to me, therefore, that before we try the tunnel I really ought to have a look for myself . . ."

There was a moist breeze laden with hints of thyme, rosemary and wet earth as Illya Kuryakin stood on the broad shelf of concrete lipping the dam later that evening. In the darkness to one side, he could hear the rustling of dry grasses where the *barrage* met the hillside. Behind him, the wind which plucked at his shirt and trouser legs stirred the water into small waves which slapped at the dam. And in front the blackness trembled as the outlets from the invisible sluices roared down the sloping face of the *barrage* in their gigantic pipes.

He was surprised to find that there appeared to be no patrolling guards on the wall of the dam itself. It had taken him three hours to work his way through whole squadrons of them deployed between the boundary fence and the shore of the lake. The hillside slopes, the ridge, the steep faces dropping to the surface of the water on the far side—all of these were stiff with armed men on the lookout. Yet here, where one might expect the concentration to be strongest, there was nobody. Nor could he hear any evidence of activity around the power station far below. It followed, therefore, that the guardians of the mysterious lake were more concerned to keep people away from the reservoir itself than from the dam forming it.

With a puzzled frown, the agent lowered himself from the lip to a small observation platform, swung from the guard rail of this to a buttress, slid down fifteen feet of rough concrete in the dark, and finally found with his feet the curved surface of the huge-bore pipe down which he intended to work his way to the power station hundreds of feet below.

Forty-five minutes later, half deafened by the tumult of falling water which had battered his ears from the other side of the conduit, he thankfully unstraddled the great iron tube, wiped the palms of his hands on his jeans, and stepped onto the balcony which circled the modernistic cube of the power station building.

There appeared to be no personnel guarding it. No lights gleamed through the slits of the shuttered windows or pierced the louvers on the doors. There was no watchman's cubicle beside the main entrance. The place seemed as deserted as the blank surface of the lake above which he had scanned so fruitlessly for so long. The nearest sign of life was the floodlight above the guardhouse, shining palely through the complexities of transformer and pylon from the main gates a quarter of a mile down the valley.

He edged his way around the balcony and found a door on the far side of the building from the gates. Crouching down, he drew from his hip pocket a square metal device about five inches square. He moistened the four rubber suction cups attached to its corners and clamped it firmly to the door above the lock. Then, straining every nerve in concentration, he placed one ear to the box and began with infinite care to oscillate a flat knob set flush with its surface. Presently he gave a satisfied grunt and rose to his feet. The door swung silently inwards at his touch and he vanished into the dark interior.

Something was wrong inside. At first he couldn't place it—then, over the muted, more muffled roar of the water, his trained senses gave him the answer. It was nothing positive; it was an absence that he noticed. There should have been a humming of generators, a whine from the giant turbines, a whiff of ozone in the air. But there wasn't.

Believing now firmly that the power station was totally uninhabited, Illya risked switching on a miniature but powerful flashlight. As soon as the thin beam lanced the dark, he saw why.

For whatever purpose the dam had been constructed, it wasn't that of supplying electricity to Getuliana. For apart from ducts leading the seething water direct from the pipes out to the river which wound down to the gates and the bridge, the vast building was completely empty. There were no turbines, no generators, no insulators, no railed catwalks or gauge-and-dial consoles. Like the metalled but trafficless road leading to it, the place was nothing but a blind, a colossal sham. . . .

Chapter 9

The Message That Had To Get Through

ALTHOUGH THE WALLS were damp to the touch, there seemed to be a current of dry air blowing through the cell.

Napoleon Solo had no idea how long he had been there. There was always a bright light burning and the only means he had of marking the passage of time was the doctor's visit—if indeed he was a doctor. At least he wore a white coat and he was always attended by two women in nurse's uniform. On the other hand, the visits might be sporadic and not regular at all. Certainly it seemed to Solo that there was more time now between the hypodermic injections than there had been before when he had still be strapped to the bed.

The bed was made of iron and enameled black. It was high and narrow, with a thin, hard mattress and no bedclothes, and its legs were cemented into the floor of the cell.

For a long time it had been Solo's world. Although he was not particularly uncomfortable with his wrists and ankles buckled into the leather bracelets at the four corners of the bed and his middle restrained by a broad strap passing under its frame, it nevertheless afforded him only a limited horizon. The walls of the cell were of smooth green cement; the ceiling, with its four powerful bulbs behind armored glass, was stone colored; and what little he could see of the floor looked like slate. The door was a single slab of steel without even a judas-window. And that was all—there was no furniture of any kind, no decoration to break the monotony, only a single small grille through which he imagined the warm, dry air was extracted.

In the circumstances, it was natural that he should take an abnormal interest in the bed. He knew by heart every chip and scratch and imperfection in the shiny surface of its headrail. He could have mapped with his eyes closed the graining of the leather handcuffs attaching his wrists to the frame. He was an authority on the disparate personalities of three flies and a daddy-longlegs in the cell whose existence was dedicated to avoiding the webs spun by a spider which lived in one corner of the grille.

Every now and then the door would swing silently open and in would come the doctor with his crisp, white women. The women varied but the doctor was always the same—a pudding-faced man, rather plump, with staring brown eyes behind thick spectacles.

One of the women would open a case and hand things to the doctor while the other put the heel of her hand under Solo's chin and forced his head back onto the mattress so that he couldn't raise himself. Then the doctor would pinch up a fold of skin from Solo's arm (so far as he could tell, he had been stripped to his underwear and socks) and inject whatever it was he injected. After that, Solo went to sleep.

This routine wasn't invariable, of course: there were different treatments too, involving tubes and clips and something like a dentist's gag. It was to do with food or feeding, Solo thought. Sometimes there was a clip biting into his arm with a tube attached to it, and sometimes something went into his throat. In either case, it left him rather sore—and in each case he usually went to sleep afterwards just the same.

The man and the two women always worked in complete silence, which Solo found rather unnerving at first, but his throat was always too dry and sore to ask questions or talk himself and he soon got used to it.

And yet there *was* talking, somewhere. Or there had been. And one of the voices, he could almost have sworn, was his own. Yet he could in no way remember talking or think of anything to talk about. Perhaps he dreamed while he slept, but he had definite impressions of voices and movement, the words surging and receding like bees on a drowsy summer afternoon. Some time or other, too, there had been someone shouting. Perhaps it had been him.

It was all very puzzling.

And then, suddenly, one day—one night? one morning? one afternoon? he could not tell—one day the doctor had come in with his two assistants and they had unbuckled the straps and taken them away. He was left alone in the cell, free to get up, sit down, move around, just as he liked.

Solo thought that was very kind. He was so grateful that he made no protest when they came back a little later to give him another injection.

It was funny about the injections. Really he felt quite giddy after them sometimes. Everything seemed to spin around and he could never tell if he really *had* been to sleep or whether perhaps he had actually just woken up from the time before. Sometimes he thought he had been in the cell for weeks, perhaps months; and sometimes he was convinced he had only been in there a few hours at the most and would soon begin to feel hungry.

On the whole, he was inclined to favor the former theory—mainly because one of the nurses, a pretty one he had noticed on several visits, seemed to have had different hairstyles on different occasions.

He remembered who he was—and what he was supposed to be doing—in a single blinding moment of awareness. The doctor and the nurses were just coming in, the cell door had opened . . . and there was a sec-

94

ond's delay. Somebody outside had called a question to the doctor.

And in the instant that he replied, over the mumble of voices, somewhere down the passage outside a door slammed sharply.

As it shut, a door in Napoleon Solo's mind opened as suddenly. Every detail of his life up to the moment he had realized that the carafe in the hotel room at Goiás had been drugged was with him again. It was exactly as though the preceding period really had been a confused and disturbing dream from which now suddenly he was freshly awake.

"How long have I been held here under sedation and artificially induced amnesia?" he asked quietly as the doctor approached.

"*Ah! The moment of breakthrough has come and gone, then*"—the voice came not from the doctor but in a curiously disembodied way from the grille which extracted the breathed air in the cell—"*and Mr. Solo knows once more just who he is! . . . Never mind: perhaps we have been fortunate to have had him for our . . . guest . . . for so long.*"

"You haven't answered my question," the agent said, still facing the doctor.

"*Doctor Gerhardi is not permitted to speak with you, Mr. Solo,*" the voice continued. "*You may talk to me. After all, we are old friends.*"

"I'm afraid you have the advantage of me," Solo said, swinging around to face the grille and feeling rather foolish as he did so. "Or have we held—er—conversations while I have been drugged?"

A deep chuckle floated from the grating. "*'Have the advantage' is good,*" the voice said. "*You might almost call us intimates. Through the closed-circuit television camera mounted behind one of the four lighting panels in your ceiling, you have been under constant watch since the moment you arrived. And thanks to the doctor's persuasionary powers you have been most cooperative in the matter of conversations.*"

"You have been questioning me under the influence of Pentathol?"

"A refined version of a drug discovered centuries ago by the Matto Grosso Indians—a drug which makes Pentathol seem as mild and innocuous as an aspirin. So far as information goes, Mr. Solo, you have been sucked as dry as a lemon! Now it only remains to decide whether the rind shall be discarded or whether it might add zest to a cocktail by being shaved and twisted. . . . There is no point in proceeding with the injection at this time, doctor: once the amnesiac condition has been broken through, one has to go right back to the beginning again."

"I trust you obtained the information you wanted," Solo said politely.

"Indeed, yes. Indeed. We know all we want to know, now, about the United Network Command for Law and Enforcement, and why Mr. Waverly sent you out here, and what Mr. Forster of the C.I.A. said, and so on."

"Nonsense. I don't believe it!" Solo said.

All Enforcement Agents from U.N.C.L.E. were periodically "brainwashed" by a system of subliminal suggestions which was supposed to plant in their minds a series of conditioned answers to any questions they might be asked when under the influence either of drugs or of torture. The theory was that it was best to give as much as possible of the truth, particularly as regards the agent's affiliation with the Command and so on: after all, any adversaries might already know this, and any untruths there would automatically invalidate further revelations. On the other hand, if a victim first confirmed what the questioners knew, they would be all the more likely to believe what he said subsequently. A mental "censor" was supposed to operate on the agent's mind as soon as the questions genuinely impinged on the task in hand—and from that point the prepared lies were supposed to operate subconsciously, even under the deepest hypnosis. It was therefore essential for Solo to know whether this system had worked—and the only way he could find out was to discover from his captors what they had been told while he was under their drugs.

"What do you mean, you don't believe it?" the voice was asking.

"I told you," Solo said. "You can't have got any information from me when I was drugged. We are conditioned. You could have found out I belonged to the Command, and about Waverly, from many sources."

"We could have, perhaps. But we didn't. You told us everything. Absolutely everything."

"Ridiculous!" Solo said contemptuously. "I simply do not believe you."

"I tell you, you came across with the whole works." There was a definite edge to the voice now. "You're not imbecilic, Mr. Solo. There is no need to bandy words. You can believe me when I tell you—"

"And I tell you I don't believe you. It's just a trick— and a very old and shabby trick, too, like telling a man his confederate has confessed all—to make him talk."

"You have talked, Solo. Plenty. So much so that there's no point—no need, for God's sake!—to ask you anything more. We have it."

"Rubbish," Solo said shortly. He turned away from the grille and sat down on the bed. The pretty nurse flashed him a knowing smile as she went out with the doctor and her colleague.

"Do you want me to prove it to you, for Heaven's sake?" the voice cried.

"Prove it? You couldn't. Not in a million years," Solo gibed.

"No? . . . Not if I told you we knew you came to Brazil because of the fingerprints of those D.A.M.E.S. women in the car crash? Not if I told you everything about your conversations with Garcia, your visit to the hospital and the discovery of the old man Oliveira? Not if I detailed the things the boy at the rental company said—the one with the old-fashioned slang? . . . Not even if I listed your findings so far in the hunt to discover the places where these false D.A.M.E.S. are distributing the cocaine and heroin?" There was a hint of laughter in the voice.

Napoleon Solo mentally heaved a sigh of relief. The built-in censor had worked. Under the drugs, he had told them every mechanical step he had taken in the investigation—but the subliminal suggestions had taken over when it had come to the reasons for the inquiry.

He had said that U.N.C.L.E. thought the girls were connected with some drug ring. His captors would believe that: the Command did interest itself in illegal drug traffic and the facts as known to Solo could believably be interpreted as leading to that erroneous conclusion.

The man who had been interrogating him would be laughing at the thought of Solo's gullibility, thinking he had wrested from the agent all he knew—which would leave him free to go on wondering exactly what *was* afoot.

And about this, Solo reflected ruefully, he knew very little.

"*You look crestfallen, my friend,*" the voice was saying jubilantly. "*I told you I could prove it! . . . Oh well, never mind. There has to be a loser in every game, doesn't there? . . . For the moment, until we decide what is to be done with you, you can take a little rest—on our laurels!*" There was a dry chuckle and the sound of a switch snapping off.

The agent threw himself on the bed and gazed moodily at the ceiling. After a while, he turned over a lay face downwards, with his chin pillowed on crossed arms. If they were really leaving him alone for a while, there was a chance the television camera above him might be switched off as well as the two-way speaker grille. Especially if he appeared as despondent as possible.

It was while he was lying perfectly still like that, hoping his negative mime might have some positive effect, that he felt something under the tightly drawn mattress covering that had certainly not been there before . . . a foreign body that was irregular in shape, sharp at the edges, and extremely hard.

And suddenly he remembered that last glance the prettier of the nurses had thrown him. Hadn't she been swiveling her eyes in a meaningful sort of way at this corner of the room? And, now that he came to think of it, hadn't that parting gaze been the last of several? Had she not been continually staring over at the bed today?

Carefully, slowly, in case he was still being watched by the camera, he slid one hand beneath the cover. In a few moments, he had it back under his chin with something small and metallic grasped in it. There were several separate objects under the cover—and not until he had withdrawn all of them did he drop his eyes and look at what lay beneath the protective wall of his cupped palm.

Four small stainless steel instruments lay on the bed: a nail file, a scalpel, an implement like a crochet hook with a sharp point, and a thin, flexible spatula.

Solo stared at them unbelievingly. Why had the girl left them there?

With a combination of two of them, he could probably pick the lock of the cell door. If the spatula was strong enough and flexible enough, he might even be able to slip the tongues without picking it.

Could the girl possibly have known this?

If not, what a curious coincidence that she should leave just the particular tools that could be used successfully to master this particular lock. On the other hand, even if she had known it, why leave him the means to escape from the cell?

He would puzzle it out later, he thought: the thing now was to find out if he was still watched—and therefore whether or not he could safely make use of this gift from Heaven. After a few moments, he decided that the best thing was simply to sit up on the bed holding the tools in full view of the camera. If it was switched on, someone would come through the door soon enough to take them away from him; if it was off, nothing would happen and he could get to work on the lock. In either case, he lost nothing—for he could never use the implements if the TV circuit *was* still on. . . .

After sitting for some time with the shining steel things in his hand, he decided that at last his luck had changed. No sound came through the grille; no footsteps clattered in the passage outside; nobody burst into the cell.

In three strides, he was at the steel door, his fingers busy twisting, probing, manipulating. He slid the spatula between the edge of the door and the jamb, testing the tongues and the resilience of their springs. It couldn't be opened with the spatula alone, that was for sure —perhaps the slender point of the scalpel, aided with a little extra leverage from the file *here* . . . Ah! There was the slight rolling movement of a tumbler beginning to fall.

He paused with the two instruments inserted, one supporting the other, into the keyhole. No matter how he turned, the wretched thing would not quite overcome its nul-point and drop.

But of course—that was what the crochet hook was for! He fed the shaft in, questing delicately with the curved point. It was extremely tricky feeling about blind with this while keeping up the complementary pressure on the other two instruments with his left hand. But eventually he sensed the satisfying *chuck!* of the wards falling home. The door should now be unlocked and ready to open.

He pulled with his fingertips at the edge. The door would not move.

Puzzled, he squinted into the crack by the lock. . . . Of course! This was the Mark III. He had moved back the retaining bars, but the tongues were still grooved into their steel nests in the jamb. It needed a gentle pressure to push them aside—and *that*, naturally, was what the spatula was for!

He eased the flat blade into the crack and worked at it with his wrist. One after the other, the greased metal bars slid silently back into the body of the lock.

The door swung slowly open.

Outside, a dimly lit passage stretched away in each direction. There were closed doors like the one he had just opened on either side, and flush fitting lamps in the ceiling every few yards. From somewhere beyond the righthand branch of the corridor, machinery hummed quietly. Feeling faintly ridiculous in singlet and underpants, Solo tiptoed on stockinged feet towards the sound.

Around the bend in the passage the girl was waiting. His breath hissed in with surprise as he saw her—but then he realized she had a welcoming smile on her face and he breathed out in a long, slow sigh of relief. She had taken off the white nurse's uniform and now she was dressed in the D.A.M.E.S. green. Her lips were parted in a smile but her eyes, shadowed by a bang of blonde hair, were troubled.

"I thought you were never coming," she whispered. "What happened? I thought you were supposed to be a top agent!"

"I had to wait to make sure the TV was off before I started on the lock," Solo whispered back. "But I don't get it. What gives? Why would you help me escape?"

"I hated my foster parents," the girl murmured. "They used to keep birds in cages. When I was eight I set most of them free. The old man half killed me—and ever since then I've always hated to see anything in captivity. Setting things free is my way of getting even, I guess. . . . I suppose that's why I married Danny."

"Danny?"

"Danny Lerina. Greatest safe man on the Coast. There wasn't a lock made that he couldn't master."

"Wasn't?"

"He was killed on some government job in Korea— but not before he'd taught me most of what he knew. Come to think of it, you're a little like him, you know. Maybe that's why I kind of took a shine to you when I saw you in there."

"Well, thanks," Solo said softly. "But tell me—just what's going on in here? Where is this place? What's happening? . . . Forgive my interrupting—we can continue the mutual admiration society afterwards, and I think you're pretty, too—but first I'd like to know where I am!"

"Gee, I'm sorry. Of course. Here, put these on." She produced a rolled up dungaree suit from under her arm. "It's not much but it was all I could get in the time. I'll talk while you dress."

"Shouldn't we go somewhere—ah—quieter?"

"What for? We're on C Level down here—just the cells, the stores, some of the minor offices, and the reactor."

"Did you say reactor?"

"Sure. It's only a little one, of course—but since the

power station outside the dam's a blind, we have to get power from somewhere, don't we?"

"I—ah—I guess so, yes. What about the offices, though —isn't somebody likely to be in and out of them?"

"At three-thirty in the morning?"

"Oh . . . I'm sorry. I'd no idea. I thought it was just after lunch time!"

The girl laughed. "No, I suppose you could hardly know, down here," she said. "Not that it's much different on B and A, for that matter."

"And what does one find on B and A?"

"Well, living quarters on B, of course. And catering. And the important offices and the Council Chamber. And the radio room and the armory. The barracks . . . and so on. A Level's mainly the pen, of course—"

"The pen?"

"Yes, the pen. For the ship. It has to go somewhere, doesn't it?"

"There's a ship connected with this place—and the ship docks on the *top* story? Presumably A Level *is* the upper one?"

"Yes, yes. For the depth. They can't risk her grounding, you know."

"I *don't* know!" Solo burst out. "Look, just to please me, tell me what's going on here. I assume we're still somewhere near the dam . . . right? Well, I know about the dam itself, I know about the power station that doesn't work, I know there's about twenty miles of valley filled up by an artificial lake. I know Getuliana's as much a blind as the hydroelectric scheme and the made-up road that leads from one to the other. But that's all I know. I don't know what's going *on*."

"Well the pen's on the top floor because the whole place is under water and—"

"Under *water!*"

"Of course. Didn't you know that? . . . Well, obviously you didn't or you wouldn't look so surprised. Yes, while they were building the dam they also built this place on the floor of the valley, completely covered in and watertight—and then when it was finished and the water rose it was eventually covered over."

"How do you get in and out?"

"There's a tunnel that leads to it through the mountain. It comes out in the next valley at the estancia. And of course you can get in and out through the pen—though that doesn't do you much good, since the ship only comes back to the same place; there's no other dock in the lake."

"And where do you girls come in? Why the D.A.M. E.S.?"

"We helped resettle the natives from the valley, and—"

"I know that, but why not real D.A.M.E.S. for that matter?"

"I suppose because we had to become members of Thrush—for the secrecy, you know—and they felt we'd be more likely to agree if we had police records. All of us have, you know. I guess they pretended we belonged to this organization just in case any Brazilian officials asked about us—just to keep the thing looking aboveboard. And then again, they preferred West Coast girls because of the swimming."

"The swimming?"

"We all had to be good swimmers and divers—divers especially. To help with the ship in the pen."

"Do you mean to say," Solo asked, the light finally bursting, "that the pen is under water too? It's an underwater dock . . . the ship is a submarine?"

"But of course, I thought you realized."

"They go to all this trouble to find spurious reasons to construct an artificial lake—just so they can build an underwater dock and play submarines with it? Why?"

The girl told him.

Solo gave a long, low whistle of astonishment. "Look," he said, "I don't know how you think we can get out of this watery fortress—"

"I don't think we can. It's just that I don't like to see people in cells. I told you."

"Sure. Well, never mind that. The point is—in or out, I have to make contact with my boss. You don't have any objection? . . . I mean, you don't appear to have any particularly strong allegiance to Thrush."

"I couldn't care less. Not if they keep people in cells."

"Sure, sure. It's a thing you have. I know. . . . Now, did I hear you say there was a radio room here? If so, it seems my best plan would be to try and crash that first and send a message from here, rather than try to escape from the place altogether—which is probably impossible —and make contact from outside. Do you agree?"

"Yes. I think there's only one man left on duty at night. And I don't suppose he'll be too alert at this time—but you watch out. You don't have too much reserve of strength, you know: you've been under heavy sedation for days."

"Just show me where the radio room is," Solo said, "and I'll worry about my strength when we get there. I promise not to kill more than a hundred of them. . . ."

The girl took his arm and led him through a maze of passages, past louvered doors shaking with the vibrations of unseen machinery, past notice boards winking with red pilot lights and green and blue, and up a flight of concrete stairs winding around a shaft housing three elevators. On the level above, the humming of the plant was less obtrusive—though he still found the windowless subterranean atmosphere, with its dry and hygienic air, oppressive in the extreme. Somewhere below them, beneath the massive foundations of the fortress, lay the drenched earth which had until so recently supported the footsteps of simple farmers; somewhere around and above, millions of tons of water pressed remorselessly in upon the walls.

And somewhere not far away must be the heads within whose crania lay the warped brains which had conceived the evil plan which Napoleon Solo alone could thwart.

If he was lucky!

The doors on the higher level were mostly glass-paned and Solo saw as they passed offices with desks, a library with rows of filing cabinets, a computer room bright with levers and dials and lights, a miniature lecture theater where the semicircle of seats surrounded a vast wall map whose rash of bulbs and flags concentrated around the newly filled-in shape of the lake.

Finally the girl drew him against the wall and put her lips to his ear. "The first door around the corner of the passage is the radio room," she whispered. "There's probably only one man there at this time, as I say—but the Council Chamber is immediately beyond, and the main control room lies between the two, only further in, as it were. . . . So there may be lots of other people within call."

"I don't know why you should do all this for me, Mrs. Lerina—"

"You can call me Alice."

"Alice, then—thank you. I don't know why you should risk your life like this for me—but I'll try to make it up to you if ever we get out of here. . . . Are you actually on duty tonight? Could you have some reason for walking past the radio room door?"

"Sure I could. You want me to find out who's there, is that it?"

"It would help, Alice."

"Okay," the blonde said. "You want I should try and get the guy to come outside?"

"I don't think so. There may be other people who can overhear. If you could go past and signal to me afterwards . . ."

"Will do," the girl said. She walked on around the corner of the passage, with Solo sidling after her like a disembodied shadow. Beyond the right-angle, the corridor was wider, with rubber floor tiles in marbled gray. Halfway along, a shaft of bright light barred the gloom by an open door. Alice Lerina walked up and paused, looking into the room.

"Hi, there!" she said. "You all on your lonesome?"

"Like usual on this trick," a man's voice replied over the faint burble of automatic morse. "I'm waiting for a call to come through from some guy he has a report to make from Zurich, Switzerland. You wanna come on in and share the solitude?"

"I don't mind. Watcha got there, anyway?" The girl stepped across the threshold, trailing behind her one arm with which she gave Solo first the thumbs-up sign, then a single finger pointing upwards.

Taking this to mean that the man was alone and that it would be safe to approach, the agent tiptoed up and

105

peered cautiously around the door. The room was small, but it was packed with chassis after chassis, console upon console of the most advanced electronic equipment Solo had ever seen. On the far side, bent over the dials of a short-wave receiver, the blonde and the operator had their backs to him. "Now this filter slope here, see," the man was saying; "with this you can tune out . . ."

There was a small monitor speaker above the set from which bursts of static occasionally sputtered. Under cover of this, Solo flitted across the room until he was immediately behind the man.

He didn't know whether it was the small current of movement he made in the dry air, or whether the girl inadvertently made some telltale sign—but a sixth-sense warning jerked up the man's head before he was within striking distance. He was a big fellow, a brawny, blue-jowled man in a singlet and uniform trousers, but he moved fast. He was on his feet facing the agent, having intercepted a glance between Solo and the girl, before Solo could raise an arm.

"Why, you dirty little . . ." he began, glowering at the blonde.

Solo's fist caught him in the solar plexus. It was essential that the man should not shout or cry out, that any struggle should be as silent as possible. Once anyone else's attention was attracted, Solo's plan would be ruined.

The operator doubled forwards with a grunt of astonishment and pain. His lips drew back from his teeth as he straightened, tugging at a blackjack in his waistband. Before he could draw enough breath back into his savaged lungs to yell, Solo had to disarm and then silence him.

Wheezing, with his eyes streaming, the man lurched forwards. Solo chopped viciously down, flat-handed, at his wrist and the blackjack clattered to the floor. At the same time, the agent raked a stinging blow across the bridge of the man's nose with the back of his other hand and thudded one stockinged heel to his kneecap. In his weakened state, Solo's only card was surprise—and he had to play it for all he was worth before the big operator could recover his equilibrium and get to close quarters.

The agent dodged back from a roundhouse left but was unable to avoid the followup—a short, pounding right that carried all the man's weight and slammed into his body just below the heart.

Solo heard his own choked grunt of pain as his legs abruptly turned to rubber and he collapsed backwards onto a wooden chair. Still groaning for breath, the operator pounced: grabbing a handful of dungarees, knuckling himself a firm hold and hauling Solo to his feet, he smashed his other fist to the agent's jaw.

Through the roaring blackness that threatened to engulf him, Solo saw dimly the huge fist drawn back again, the great face poised menacingly behind. With his remaining strength, he reached desperately up and grasped the man's ears. Then he went suddenly limp and dragged his adversary's head down after him. The man, caught momentarily off balance, pitched forwards, his hands flew instinctively out to break his fall, and his forehead crashed into a bank of equipment behind the chair.

Using the seat for leverage, Solo executed a kind of half back somersault and brought his knee jarringly up to connect with the underneath of the operator's chin as he hauled down on the ears. There was a sudden cessation of movement and then he was smothered in the dead weight of the man's unconscious body.

Panting, Solo laboriously hauled himself out from underneath with the help of the girl. Brief though it had been, the fight had totally exhausted him. Alice Lerina had been right—it would be some time before he regained his strength.

There would be no question of his attempting any further trials of strength, he realized bitterly as he dragged himself across the room to a transmitter. He must do what he had to do and worry about any subsequent action when the need for it arose. Slumping into a chair, he began methodically testing switches and revolving dials. Behind him, the girl watched wide-eyed.

It must have been almost twenty minutes later, and

the agent's labored breathing had settled down to a steadier and quieter rhythm as he concentrated on his work, when a section of wall behind them swung silently aside to reveal three men standing there.

"All right, you—away from that transmitter. *Move!*" The words cracked out from the thin mouth of the man in the middle.

Solo whirled away from the radio. The man had slender, almost feminine hands with dirty nails and cigarette-stained fingers. A half-smoked cigarette drooped soggily from one corner of his mouth. And a short-barreled P.38 hung negligently from his right hand.

Behind him were a tall, white-haired Negro with a lined face, and a well-dressed man whom Solo recognized as Wassermann, the holder of the concession to build Getuliana and the dam, whom he had met in Brasilia.

"Don't do anything foolish, Mr.—er—Williams . . . or should I say Solo?" Wassermann drawled. "Greerson may look a little lackadaisical, but it's deceptive, I assure you."

Solo stood perfectly still, his hands at his sides. A few feet away, the girl crouched above the unconscious body of the radio engineer in a pose that was almost a caricature of guilty surprise. Apart from a sharp intake of breath when Greerson had first spoken, she had remained completely silent.

"I am most surprised to find you abusing our hospitality, Mr. Solo," the Negro said. "And disappointed. I had thought you were one of our more cooperative guests." The voice, Solo realized as soon as the man spoke, was the one he had been talking to over the intercom in his cell.

"Unfortunately," Wassermann said, "we were not attending to our monitor speakers in the control room, otherwise we'd have noticed earlier that clandestine messages were being transmitted. We have, however, heard enough to tell us that you were speaking in code —and that this story of you investigating some drug racket is false."

"Most interesting," the Negro said. "I'd be fascinated to learn the details of the treatment to which you were

108

subjected. A system which permits deliberate lies to be told, mixed in with a judicious amount of truth, even under the deepest hypnosis and the most powerful drugs —that is something I really admire! Regrettably, though, I have to deny myself the pleasure of forcing you to tell me: our operation is ready to start. You have transgressed the laws of hospitality and now you have become merely an embarrassment. You must be disposed of."

"Didn't they teach you not to end sentences with a preposition in the mail-order English course you took?" Solo said blandly.

The Negro smiled. "I am immune to insults, my friend," he said. "As I was saying, you must now die. You have until darkness tomorrow night . . . tonight, I should say, for it must be almost dawn now."

"Isn't that—ah—untraditional?" Solo said. "It's usually dawn."

"It is a question of method, Mr. Solo," Wassermann said. "We like to be tidy; we do not like to arouse the curiosity of our Brazilian hosts. So any deaths that are necessary are customarily arranged to look like accidents —a hit-and-run road accident, a heart attack, that sort of thing."

"What about the girls in the car?"

"One of the troubles about employing members of the underworld is that they will not obey rules," Wassermann said. "Despite our orders, individual members of our team persisted in driving all the way down to Rio to amuse themselves in their spare time. This particular pair drove carelessly, that is all. Then they had to be silenced to ward off your prying questions. . . . In the case of your own death, as I was saying, this will be arranged to look like an accidental drowning. And it is better to stage that in darkness, simply to avoid possible witnesses."

"And how do you propose to stage it?"

"We don't really have to bother. The submarine pen attached to this building has double doors—so that the craft can enter underwater, wait until the water has been extracted, and then disgorge its crew in safety. With you, the process will be the reverse: you will be left in the pen when it is air-filled, the inner doors will close, the outer doors will open and the water will come in. And then, some time later, your body will float to the surface in the normal way and will no doubt be discovered at some time in the future by a worthy peasant. This way, too, we avoid any marks of violence on the body."

"Bodies—not body," the Negro put in. "We cannot tolerate disloyalty." He walked across the room to the girl. "You could have seriously jeopardized our plans by helping this man," he said with cold malice. "Now you will have to pay for your foolishness with your life." He raised his arm and slapped her repeatedly, forehanded and backhanded, across the face. The marks of his fingers stood out lividly against the girl's pallor as a thread of blood crawled slowly down her chin from one corner of her mouth.

"All right, Hernando, that's enough," Wassermann said. "No, Mr. Solo—I wouldn't. I really wouldn't. . . . Greerson, you'd better calm Mr. Solo down before we take him back to his cell with his fellow conspirator to await the night, eh?"

"Okay," the man called Greerson said. He handed his gun to Wassermann and shambled forwards across the room, his baggy suit flapping on his bony frame. "Only thing is," he said as he approached the agent, "my hands are kinda delicate and I hate to bruise them. You know?"

Solo automatically raised his arms to defend himself as Greerson came near. But the thin man took him by surprise. Moving like lightning, his left hand reached out and grasped Solo's shoulder, spinning him deftly around so that he was facing the wall. Then, almost in the same movement, the gunman's other fist looped in and buried itself in Solo's kidney.

The agent's fingers scrabbled at the concrete wall as he sank to the ground, a strangled cry forcing itself from his lips. Dimly through waves of nausea he heard the girl cry out—though whether in pain or in horror at what was happening to him he did not know.

Behind him, Greerson measured his distance carefully, then drew back his foot. . . .

Chapter 10

"Don't Call Us—We'll Call You! . . ."

As Greerson raised his foot in the fortress below the artificial lake, Illya Kuryakin turned the key to cut the motor of the Volkswagen fourteen hundred yards away on the other side of the rocky spur separating the reservoir from the adjoining valley.

Mist clung to the lower branches of the trees like streamers of chiffon, blanketed the hollows in the ground, and wreathed in frightening shapes across the road. The estancia was invisible in the before-dawn darkness as he coasted the car in under some overhanging evergreens opposite the gates. Beside him, the greyhound profile of Coralie Simone was pale and tense in the dim illumination of the single dashboard light.

"Somewhere in that mountain," Illya said, "there is a kind of fortress where all those trucks full of material go. It must lie at the end of the tunnel—though whether it is on this side of the lake or beyond it we can't tell. Since we couldn't possibly identify the place from above —even if the guards allowed us enough time on the shores of the lake to try—we'll just have to force our way in through the tunnel. Because somewhere in there, dead or alive, is Napoleon Solo . . . It'll be dawn in about a half hour: it seems to me that now is as good a time as any to try. Are you game?"

"So far as this phase of the operation is concerned," the girl said, "you are the boss. If you say go, we go."

"Fine. Well, the first thing to do is to spy out the land. Just hold on a moment while I fix the equipment, will you?"

Kuryakin hauled an attaché case over from the car's back seat and took out what looked like a heavy flashlight with a hooded lens. He held the device out of the VW's window and pressed the switch. There was no result at all—until he and the girl looked through a pair of viewfinders resembling truncated field glasses. Then the darkened and misty topography sprang to life in a manner as quick as it was impressive. In the powerful infrared beam cast by the flashlight, the special lenses showed up trees, grasses, fences, gateposts and buildings as vividly and dramatically as though they had been the snow scene they resembled.

"Oh, it's beautiful," the girl cried. "It looks just like full moon—only much brighter!"

Illya's face remained impassive. "Seems quiet enough," he said. "I guess we'd better get moving while it's still dark out there. Unless we can penetrate the tunnel mouth before dawn, we might as well go home."

While the girl held the infra-red lamp out of the passenger window, Kuryakin strapped the lenses over his eyes and got out of the car. He crossed the road and busied himself with the latch of the wire gates blocking the entry to the estancia. In the unearthly light visible to him through his glasses, it took him less than thirty seconds to pick the lock. There seemed to be no alarm system connected with it. The gate was used so much that they probably considered the alarms were best left further inside the Thrush enclave.

When he had swung the gates open, he ran lightly back across the road and released the handbrake of the car.

"Here, take one of these guns," he said crisply to the girl, rummaging again in the attaché case. "Basically, as you see, they're long-barreled .32 automatics—too big for the pocket but splendid for using in a car. The great thing about them, however, is the accessory department: look, you can screw on, separately or together, a shoulder stock, a barrel extension with silencer that gives them greater accuracy, a butt extension that means you can use them two-handed from the hip, and an infra-red viewfinder. That means you can see the light thrown by this flashlight for aiming—but you don't have to bother about wearing special glasses."

"I can't wait!" Coralie exclaimed, taking the spidery-looking weapon gingerly and examining it carefully.

"I'm serious," Kuryakin said. "You may have to use it if you're with me. . . . In the meantime: let's go!"

Standing outside the open driver's door with one hand on the wheel, he began to push. Slowly the car began to move, gathering momentum as it left the grassy shoulder and rolled across the highway, moving still faster as the tires crunched on gravel and it passed the gateposts, accelerating at last as the wheels ran down the gentle slope leading towards the screen of bushes and the tunnel mouth. As soon as the vehicle had enough momentum, Illya swung into the seat and steered from the inside, his eyes probing the space behind every bush in the weird illumination provided by the infra-red lamp and the glasses.

The Volkswagen, without a light showing and with a dead motor, sped down the incline in the darkness, twisting past bushes and obstructions with unerring aim.

The dregs of the night hung heaviest in the wooded hollow just before the entrance to the tunnel. Taking her eye away for a moment from the infra-red light, the girl was astonished to see how stygian the blackness was. Very dimly, now, she could make out the darker blur that was the cliff face, the indistinct opening of the tunnel mouth. From here, too, she could faintly make out the double row of low-power ceiling bulbs that marked the course of the subterranean passage curving away into the heart of the hill.

Kuryakin's plan was to switch on the ignition, put the car in gear and then let in the clutch to start the engine once they were inside the tunnel. He only needed the surprise brought by silence to get past any guards and keep the car rolling. From there on, he intended to roar through the tunnel as fast as he could, trusting again to that element of surprise to enable him to get through and establish a position on the far side before any of the defenders had realized what was happening.

After that, he would have to play it by ear. He only hoped that fate would allow him to consolidate a position strong enough at least to bargain from. If not, his

113

own position—and the girl's—would be as bad, if not worse, than Solo's.

Still—he had to try. There was nothing else he could do.

Coralie was looking through the gunsight again now, squinting along the barrel at the strange lunar landscape thrown into relief by the magic beam of the flashlight in her other hand. She idly scrutinized the shadowed interstices of the cliff face, glanced at the trees standing proud like cardboard cutouts against the rock, looked past the closed door to the guardhouse, and up at the arched tunnel mouth—

"*Illya!*" she screamed. "*Look out! The tunnel . . . Stop!*"

Tires screeched as he stamped on the pedal to lock the car's back wheels. The great steel shutter that she had glimpsed rumbling down to seal off the entrance slammed home in its metal guides. The VW, slowing but not able to stop entirely in the time, slid straight into it with a noise like a hundred thunderclaps.

"We must have crossed a photo-electric cell guard," Kuryakin shouted as he started the engine, crashed the gearshift into reverse and backed the buckled car away from the blanked off tunnel mouth. "That thing was automatically operated or I'm—"

A burst of shooting drowned his words. Bullets thumped into the bodywork and spanged off metal projections as he screamed around in a half circle, thumped a tree bole, coaxed the car back into first and shot back the way they had come. The VW's gas tank was in the front of the car and if there was to be shooting it was better to keep it at the far end! "The light! Put the light on again!" he yelled to the girl as he wrestled with the wheel. "Nobody can see it but us!"

Coralie had, almost as a reflex, switched the flashlight off as soon as she'd seen the steel shutter crashing down. Now she thumbed the lever again and stared anxiously through the screen as Illya rocketed them up towards the house. There was nobody to be seen, although the gunfire was as intense as ever. Above the explosions, an

114

insistent, thin shrilling, an alarm bell could be heard ringing and ringing.

"Get down below the seat back!" the agent shouted. "They're firing at us from in front too, now." He zigzagged the car wildly from side to side. The windshield starred and a side window shattered. Shards of glass fell noisily to the floor.

"As I thought," he continued. "Those guns must be computer-aimed—they could never fire so accurately in the dark otherwise. Look! In the infra-red! You can see a bank of them."

The girl peered over the edge of the door and saw in the beam from the flashlight a group of muzzles belching flame and smoke from a steel screen behind a clump of bushes.

"Hold tight!" Kuryakin called. "I'll go in here: maybe the trees will slow down their radar responses." The car careened off the roadway and bumped on flat tires among the great trunks studding the woods between the tunnel and the estancia. Abruptly there was a stinging sensation in Coralie's hand and the light from the lamp dwindled and vanished. A stray slug had killed the flashlight. At the same time the motor spluttered and died; it was all very well to turn your back to preserve the tank, but that put your carburetor in a very vulnerable position.

Now that the car was silent, they could hear above the shrilling of the bell the distant shouts of orders, the trampling of feet, a door opening and slamming as men filed through. Somewhere through the trees, a searchlight dazzled on and outlined the leaves in golden light.

For a moment Kuryakin sat tense, his lower lip thrust out, his deep-set eyes glittering beneath that bulging brow. His forehead was beaded with sweat and a trickle of blood from a furrow scoring one cheekbone had dried on his face. For the moment, the shooting seemed to have stopped.

"They've halted the automatic fire to let their men move in," he said at last. "Come on! Let's go while the going's good." Seizing the girl by the hand, he pushed his way out of the riddled car and dodged away through the trees. A moment later they heard a tractor grinding along the road towards the thicket.

There was a flurry of commands and a second searchlight killed the dark just behind them. Tiger-striped with bars of blazing light, the little wood seemed suddenly a bare and empty place, the black shadows the only hints of comfort and warmth within it. There was a rattle of bolts and a volley of gunshots again. Bullets thwacked into the leaves around them and the girl heard one zing past her ear with a noise like an angry bee.

"Stay behind a tree and give me covering fire," Kuryakin cried.

As the girl turned to pump slugs from the unfamiliar U.N.C.L.E. gun in the general direction of the shouts, she saw him flit from shadow to shadow, from trunk to trunk, until he was only forty or fifty yards from the tractor. He dropped on one knee and cradled the gun to his right shoulder.

Then flame stabbed the dark as the gun leaped in his hands. A moment later, the searchlight on the tractor went out suddenly.

Kuryakin was back at the girl's side, materializing from the dark. "Come on," he whispered. "We'll get out. If they run true to form, it'll be grenades after this. Then dogs. . . . I know when I'm beaten—temporarily. We'll have to retire to lick our wounds and rethink."

There was a dull plop from behind them as they threaded their way through the undergrowth as quietly as they could. It was followed by a second, a third, a fourth. Among the tatters of mist that the approaching dawn limned white against the trees, another and more pungent vapor eddied and swirled.

"Tear gas!" Illya cried hoarsely, suppressing a cough and trying not to dab his streaming eyes. "Good thing we left in time to miss the full effect."

For a fraction of a second, the wood sprang lividly to life in the green glare of an explosion. Simultaneously, they heard the flat crump of the detonation. Metal rasped, glass tinkled and things tore through the leaves.

"Mortar," the agent said curtly, hauling himself up onto an overhanging branch and hanging motionless beside the wire fence which showed dimly in the watery lights seeping into the sky from the east. "Here—put your arms around my legs and swing yourself across. . . . It sounds as though they've disposed of the old VW for us. Next they'll start quartering the thicket before they send in the dogs."

He shifted along the branch hand over hand and dropped silently to the road.

"Lucky for us," he said, taking the girl's hand and setting off at a run, "that we thought of bringing the other VW and leaving it a hundred yards further down the road! . . ."

In San Felipe do Caiapo, one of the ill-lit houses fronted by the boardwalk boasted a larger opening linking interior and exterior than did its neighbors. This was the nearest thing the village could produce to a coffee shop, and here Illya and Coralie repaired to soothe the feelings of humiliation and defeat engendered by their dawn patrol.

"They teach us never to underestimate an enemy," Illya said ruefully as he called for the bill, "and yet we appear to do it all the time; we just never learn, it seems!" There was a bandage across his cheek and he needed a shave. The girl—despite the dry heat of what promised to be a blazing day—looked as cool and self-possessed as ever.

A waitress whose flesh cascaded in increasing convexities from chin to thigh wobbled over and handed Illya a grubby piece of paper with figures scrawled on it. Behind it was another. On this was written, in English: *Thirty-one miles ENE on the road to Brasilia is a fork with a church between the roads. Be there for midday lunch.* It was signed *Waverly.*

"Waverly!" the Russian cried. "But that's ridiculous! How could he possibly be there? . . . How could he possibly know that we're *here?*"

"Who is Waverly?" Coralie asked.

"The head of my department at the Command."

"Do you think it's some kind of trap?"

"Oh, no. If it were a fake message, it would be bound

to be too clever—you know, *too* good, too cautious and so on. The fact that it's sent openly in English, in clear, with that laconic phrasing and superb unconcern for security—that's the genuine Waverly, all right. No, what astonished me isn't to hear from him, but to hear he's there!"

"But perhaps he isn't," the girl objected. "The message tells us to be there for lunch. It doesn't say *he'll* be there too."

Illya looked at the paper again. "So it doesn't," he said. "Let's see . . . Here! Senhora! Who gave you this paper? Where did you get it?"

But the slatternly waitress, suddenly unable to understand their Portuguese, merely shrugged her vast shoulders, spread her pudgy fingers and vanished into the interior of the house muttering something or other about a boy on a bicycle.

"Never mind," Kuryakin said. "We have the perfect way of finding out." He gestured to the Volkswagen parked across the square. "By the time we've got out of here and found a stream to clean up in, there'll be just about enough time left to make it. . . ."

It was in fact nine minutes after twelve when Illya checked the figures showing on the car's odometer and said, "Here's the thirty-first mile coming up now. But I can see ahead for two or three miles and there's no sign of a fork."

"Yes," Coralie cried, "the side road we just passed coming in . . . Stop! . . . Look, it *would* be a fork if you were coming the other way, wouldn't it? And there's the church between the two roads, see!"

Illya braked and looked in the rear-view mirror. "Yes, you're right, of course," he said, turning the car on a piece of rough ground. "Thinking of the place as you come *from* Brasilia, it would never strike you that the fork wasn't one from the other direction! . . . Why, I believe it's the same junction that boy at the car rental company gave me for—"

"It is, it is," the girl interrupted. "He told me too. The signs tell you to take the right-hand road for Getuliana, but the boy said to take the left-hand one through San Felipe. Do you suppose the coffee shop there is run by his brother or something?"

"There are some misplaced hormones in the family if it is," Illya said.

"No, I don't mean the enormous lady, you idiot—Oh! What's that just to the right of the church?"

Beyond the derelict church separating the roads was a dense thicket of tall trees. A short way down the right hand fork something white and metallic glittered in a shaft of sunlight piercing the shadows.

Kuryakin drove slowly down. A huge Cadillac convertible, blinding white from stem to stern, was parked beside the road.

He coasted fifty yards past the empty car and pulled off the road. "Most of my armory went up with the other VW," he said quietly. "But I still have this Walther PPK. It's a big gun, too clumsy for whipping in and out of waistbands and pockets. . . . Do you still have your Beretta?"

The girl nodded.

"Good. You take the Walther and stay in the car to give me covering fire if necessary, and give me the Beretta to take with me, okay? . . . I'm sure it's all right, but it's better to be certain."

Coralie Simone dropped her chin to the back of the seat and watched him tread warily away among the trees, the big Walther with its brown cross-hatched butt held firmly in her small hand. The agent was grasping the Italian automatic inside the patch pocket of his lightweight jacket.

She watched him circle the Cadillac, glance at the registration number, peer inside the car, and scrutinize the trees surrounding it. Apart from the disused chapel, there wasn't another building in sight. A flock of green parakeets dipped and swooped from one side of the road to the other, and another bird, off in the thicket to her right, reiterated a harsh cry that she couldn't identify. There was a high, thin humming from the countless insects winging beneath the great leaves far above her head. Abruptly she saw Kuryakin stiffen. She brought up the gun and rested it on the seat back as he stared across the road.

The outlines of his sparse body sprang into diamond-hard relief as he stepped from the shadow to the brilliant sunlight barring the dusty surface.

"Sure 'tis over here, we are at-all, Mr. Kuryakin," the voice called from the far side of the highway. "Them blasted insects are a wee bit less attentive here for some reason—besides which we can use the extra few seconds to scrutinize the callers, eh?"

"Tufik! . . . I mean O'Rourke," Illya cried. "What the devil are you doing here, you old rascal?"

His face broke into a smile, he gestured the girl to join them, and he ran across the road. Behind a screen of flowering shrubs, the huge Irishman sat in his wheelchair at a table which had been erected in a space beneath the trees. On the white cloth covering it were plates, cutlery, glasses and plastic containers filled with food. Behind, the tall, moustached man called Raoul busied himself with a silver bucket, bottles and a portable ice-box laid out on the top of a suitcase. Four folding chairs were pulled up to the table.

"As to what we're doin' here," O'Rourke said, "well, you got the invitation, did you not? Sure, of course you did, for here you are! Well then—we're entertaining some friends to luncheon, that's what."

"Yes, but . . . It was surprising enough to hear from Waverly, but to find *you* here . . ." Illya shook his head. "Oh, I'm sorry—of course you don't know each other," he added as the girl pushed through the bushes to join them. "Manuel O'Rourke—Miss Simone. And this is a colleague of Manuel's, Coralie, whom I know only as Raoul."

"Ortiz," the moustached man smiled as he bowed and shook hands. "It is agreeable to see that now you are together and not one in pursuit of the other, eh?"

"I remember you, of course," Coralie exclaimed. "In Rio! You're the man who was following Mr. Kuryakin too, aren't you?"

"I am desolated to contradict a lady," Raoul said. "But I was actually following you."

"Come on then, let's start; let us begin," O'Rourke said. "We cannot offer you too exotic a meal, for this is peasant country, not like the coast. But there is *mungunza, acaraje,* a cucumber salad, a cold fish from the Pireneos not too unlike salmon, and *vatapá*—a Bahia dish made from manihot flour cooked with dende oil and pimentos, with slices of fish in between. Also there is a local white wine which is drinkable so long as you chill it enough to kill the flavor."

"So what about Waverly, then?" Illya asked as they sat down a few minutes later and prepared to eat.

"Waverly?"

The Russian gestured to the vacant fourth chair. "Aren't we going to wait for him?" he asked.

O'Rourke chuckled throatily. "The *vatapá* would be congealed to hell if we did," he said. "That's not Waverly's chair. That's for Rafael—he's away in the forest finding some local leaf for the salad. It's a deal of a job, you know, for 'tis not like the old country, where it's all green grasses and moss and I don't know what-all. You have to go searchin' for your greenstuff in this dried-up hole!"

"Yes, but where *is* Waverly?—if we're to take the message seriously at all."

"Waverly? Sure he's in Rio."

"Well then . . . ?"

"If we'd waited for him, stayed there until he reached us from New York, we'd not have left until this morning. So we decided to drive up yesterday and last night—it's not over six hundred miles—for the times of the planes were not convenient and anyway the car's rather—er—special."

"I'm afraid I still don't see . . ."

"Your Mr. Waverly's safe in my place. Joana and Consuela will look after him. Now come on and eat. We're not due to speak to him until two."

And not another word of business would the Irishman talk until that time. Rafael—who turned out to be the boy from the auto rental company in Brasilia—arrived with a fistful of thin green leaves. They ate and drank their way solidly through an excellently prepared and

121

served meal, and at five minutes to two, O'Rourke pushed back his wheelchair, dabbed his mouth delicately with a napkin, and said, "Right, me boyo! While Rafael and Raoul entertain the lady and prepare some coffee and Izarra, let's you and me cross the road and get to work, eh?"

The enormous trunk of the Cadillac was entirely filled with electronic equipment—transmitting, receiving and recording. As the electrically operated lid rose, Kuryakin drew in his breath with a gasp of astonishment at the sight of the valves, transistors, condensers, selectors, tuners, spools and knobbed chassis packed in there.

"Ruddy old tin can," O'Rourke said, slapping the car on one of its huge fenders. "I'd rather have an Iso Rivolta, an Aston or a Maserati. But where else would you get about ninety cubic feet of stowage and enough motor to haul all this weight?"

"It's certainly most impressive," Illya said. "But isn't this a bit public? I mean, we're right on the side of the road—"

"Have you heard any traffic while we've been eating? Did you see one single vehicle going in either direction? Tell me."

"Well, no, now that you mention it. Even so—"

"Could happen there's a roadblock a while up the road. Just a routine check, no doubt. But these things do take time . . . and sure there are so many uniforms in Brazil that it's a bold man can tell the genuine from the spurious," the Irishman said innocently.

"O'Rourke! You haven't . . . you didn't . . . Actually, you did, didn't you? You really take the cake! You seal off half a state just so that you can make a private radio contact without inconveniencing yourself! I don't see too much difference between your setup here and in Casablanca. Talk about having your cake and eating it . . ."

O'Rourke merely smiled broadly as he wheeled his chair to the rear of the car and leaned in over the open trunk, twiddling knobs and dials.

"That must be a pretty powerful combination in there," Illya said conversationally.

"Powerful? Wait'll I show you, boy. It was built for me by a fellow he got drummed out of the C.I.A. electronics research department for helping radio hams with G.I. stores. Listen . . . ?"

Through a burst of static a calm voice enunciated: *"This is the BBC Home Service. Here is the eight o'clock news. . . . The rail strike is to go on as planned. Britain's balance of payments problem was described last night as 'chaotic' by the President of San Marino. In the county cricket championship—"*

Chuckling, O'Rourke twirled his dials. *"C'est ici Radio Monte Carlo,"* a voice said loudly. *"Votre programme devedettes. Et voici l'heuro: au troisieme dop, il sera exactement . . ."*

Kuryakin looked at his watch. The minute hand was just beginning to coincide with the second hand over the hour. The hour hand stood at two.

"Hoe laat is het ontbijt? Wat hebt U klar? Wat is de specialiteit van het land?" the loudspeaker intoned. *"Vandaag, morgenochtend, altijd—het is de Corn Flakes van . . ."*

"I don't wish to seem discourteous," Illya began as a lilting German voice began to croon of loves lost and regained, "but if Waverly is expecting uus to call at two, don't you think perhaps . . . ?"

"You're right, boy. You're absolutely correct," O'Rourke said. "Here, wait'll I get the call sign going and you can speak privately on this." He handed the agent a radio-telephone receiver shaped very like the normal domestic instrument. "It's scrambled at both ends. Not to worry!"

He spoke into a microphone in the trunk, adjusting knobs. Illya heard a girl's voice speaking in Portuguese and then, after a pause, Waverly's well-known dry tones: "Mr. Kuryakin? Are you there?"

"I'm here, sir."

"Good. We have very little time. I shall try to come out there myself later today, since I've come this far. But you'll have to act on your own. At once."

"Yes, sir."

"I'll give it to you straight, a run-down from the top. Anything you've already found out, so much the better.

Afterwards you can fill me in on anything I don't know. Understood?"

"Certainly, sir. Go ahead."

"I intend to, Mr. Kuryakin. . . . First, Mr. Solo is still alive—or at least he was early this morning when he managed to reach me with a radio message. The message was interrupted, so presumably he was caught and will now be in great danger. Here's what he has discovered: Thrush used the ostensible building of a new city and a spurious hydroelectric station as a blind to get a large force of contractors into the area of San Felipe.

"Secondly, this force built a sophisticated fortress powered with atomic fuel on the floor of the valley behind the dam. When the valley was flooded to make the artificial lake supposed to supply the hydroelectric station with power, the fortress was submerged. It can now be entered only through a tunnel bored under the mountain separating the dam from the adjoining valley, or via a special underwater entrance.

"Thirdly, the false D.A.M.E.S. are a collection of women with criminal records recruited from the West Coast to help resettle and pacify those Negro and Indian peasants dispossessed through the scheme; their subsidiary tasks are to assist with certain underwater aspects of the plan.

"Fourthly, the dispossessed natives and others likely to spread gossip about the rather unorthodox procedures at San Felipe have been actively discouraged by the head of a spurious Candomblé *terreiro,* a man called Hernando, who plays upon their superstitions and invokes their gods to obtain their silence—which is why no stories of these activities seem to have reached Brasilia or Rio or Salvador.

"Fifthly, and most important, the purpose of all this: The lake has been built as a safe base for tests involving a new atomic-powered submarine, something between Polaris and Nautilus, which has been developed by Thrush scientists at the fortress."

"What!"

"In a landlocked lake far from civilization in the Matto Grosso, they can experiment on a scale impossible in the crowded seas of the world. The underwater vessel is at the moment engaged in a series of proving runs in the depths of the reservoir, but in a day or so the plan moves into its next phase—which brings me to point five. Mr. Solo tells me they plan to fire a series of intermediate-range ballistic missiles with nuclear warheads."

"What?"

"This whole operation is only a pilot scheme to give them information to be used later for plans under the oceans of the world. Even so, it involves warheads of several megatons each being launched at six cities in Argentina and Chile—Buenos Aires, Bahia Blanca, Cordoba, Santiago, Valparaiso and Concepcion, we understand. With the Pan-American conference coming up, you can readily imagine what such an attack would do to the O.A.S.!"

"But that's fantastic!" Illya exclaimed. "What can we do about it?"

"The briefing is simple," the voice in his ear said crisply. "I want you to go in there tonight and get Solo out. And at the same time I want you to put that submarine and its armaments out of action. Permanently."

"You're joking, of course," Illya said.

"Mr. Kuryakin!"

"Oh, sorry. Silly of me. You never do, do you?"

"Do you have anything constructive to say?" The voice was icy.

"Yes, sir. You cannot *get* in, for a start. . . . The reservoir fills a valley which is one of several running parallel —and the hills buttressing it on either side are too bare and too steep for wheeled vehicles. Nor can they be overlooked from anywhere: what goes on in the lake remains completely without witnesses. It's all very well chosen as a site. The only way in, as you said, is through the tunnel connecting the adjoining valley directly with the underwater fortress. But we already tried to rush that, at dawn today. And it's impossible."

"Impossible?"

"Virtually impossible. Impossible with the means I have here. You'd need a battalion of troops with medium artillery, bazookas, flame throwers and all to bust in there. The tunnel is radar-guarded with electronically operated steel shutters, computerized small arms, mortars, and so on."

"What do you suggest, then?"

"As I see it, there's only one possible plan that *could* work in the time. But it would need an awful lot of co-operation from the Command headquarters, from the U. S. or Brazilian navies, and from you, sir!"

"You can have all you want, Mr. Kuryakin. Tell me about it."

Illya spoke persuasively for three and a half minutes, put down the receiver, closed the Cadillac's trunk, and walked back across the road to the picnic. The Irishman was sipping his inevitable liqueur, telling the others an improbable story about his exploits in the Easter Rising of 1916.

"I may be calling on your services, later tonight," the Russian said when he had finished. "And anybody else who's available. Mr. Waverly has told me that you"—he turned and smiled at Coralie—"are officially in the 'to be trusted' category. And I imagine that Raoul can come wherever Senhor O'Rourke directs. But what about Rafael, here? . . . Is the car rental company yet another of your sidelines, O'Rourke?"

"Ah, now look," the fat man protested, scandalized. "Would I be likely to run a hire company? Sure I'm no businessman and you know it. Rafael earns a little money on the side by supplying me with information about clients every now and then—but he's only here with us today because it's his day off, you know. There's no professional connection!"

"Absolutely not, old boy," the boy said with his wide smile. "Simply couldn't have the staff with divided allegiances, now could we? Be a terribly bad show, too, to go for a picnic on a working day, don't you know. Must keep in with the jolly old providers, what!"

"Where in Heaven's name do you get that comic-opera English from?" Illya asked, grinning.

"But it's the latest, the very latest," Rafael protested. "Very in indeed. Mr. Williams told me."

"Mr. Williams is too busy to go to the movies often,"

Illya said gravely. "It is true that the English style *is* in—but the play-it-cool, stiff-upper-lip, drawing room manner's not the proper style. It's the so-called kitchen sink bit that's in today. The poor-but-honest, working class meritocrat—he's the man that gets the votes now."

The boy received this information with a blink of surprise, but he recovered quickly. "Whyn't you keep your flamin' lip buttoned, mate?" he said. "Straight up, you perishin' know-alls fair turn me stomach, you do!"

Chapter 11

In At The Back Door. . . .

THE SUN HAD sunk beneath the bleached rim of rock formed by the higher sierras a quarter of an hour before the giant helicopter whirred in from the east. It had been touch-and-go whether or not they got a troop-carrier but Waverly had been pulling strings in Rio and Washington all afternoon and eventually he had made it. The nearest chopper with a bomb bay had been aboard a ship somewhere off Central America, even then, and they had spent an anxious hour and a half wondering whether the pilot was going to get there in time. Eventually he had sunk onto the runway at Brasilia and explained that he had thought it best to bring the ship with him rather than trust to another plane. Waverly—who had been sitting up front with the pilot—had nodded exasperatingly in agreement.

And now the operation was at last under way. Waverly had driven off in the Cadillac with O'Rourke and Raoul and Rafael—who had refused point-blank to be left out of it—and was to wait within transceiver call of the tunnel in case they might be able to fight their way out and could use assistance.

Illya and Coralie, gleaming in skin-tight suits of black rubber, sat just behind the double doors of the bay. In front of them, the midget submarine with its perspex blisters lay sleekly in its specially rigged davits. It looked as frail and crushable as the fabric of the aircraft itself in the faint light drifting back from the instruments showing through the half-open door of the cockpit. Presently the copilot emerged from the cabin and shut the door. He sat down next to Illya and began to speak. He was a navy man, crewcut, with a Bostonian accent.

"Just to check out the details with you people," he said, "I'd like to repeat, one, that you take your places and we screw you down before we lose height at twenty-seventeen. You've already been briefed on how to release the hatches from inside. Two, we shall set her down to within about twenty feet of the surface and then lower away. You'll have to be prepared to get bumped if there's anything of a breeze down there, anything enough to make a wave on that lake. Three, in her present trim, it would be most unwise to go lower than about forty fathoms—this hasn't the depth capability of that Squid you used on your last assignment,* and we didn't have time to fly the Squid here for you. Besides, it wouldn't have worked in this lake—it's fresh-water, not salt-water. How far below the surface is this underwater pen, d'you know?"

"We have no idea," Illya said. "Deep enough, obviously, for the buildings to escape detection from the air."

"Well, even with nearly vertical sides and good camouflage, that would need a good twenty to thirty fathoms to the *top* of the buildings."

"I know. We'll just have to hope the entry to the pen is on an upper floor, that's all! The place is built up from the floor of the old valley of course, but we don't know yet how many stories there are."

"I see. Now, what else? Oh, yes: radar. The equipment's the usual gear, handled by the back-marker. There's not much room in there, as you can see, but there's a miniature aqualung each. If you do have to get out, though, remember you have only thirty minutes of oxygen in them. Now I have to ask you a question. Number One wants to know: Do they have any AI at all? Can they spot a UFO and if so will they open up? It's

---

*See THE MAN FROM U.N.C.L.E. #8, *The Monster Wheel Affair*.

a question of being prepared to take evasive action," he said apologetically.

"We don't *know*," Illya said. "Our whole scheme is predicated on the assumption that they don't. Having taken all this trouble to build a secret place where nobody can observe them, making their *own* sea to sail on as it were, we imagine they'll feel secure enough not to have bothered. No scheduled air corridors cross the region and we can see no reason for them to have guarded against air or water invasion—in the first place, there's nothing for a plane to see; and in the second, how can there be any other craft on the lake when it's just been made and their underwater base is the only dock on it? . . . All the same, to be honest, we don't actually know. And if they can tape planes, they'll be on to us!"

"We'd better keep our fingers crossed for each other, then, hadn't we?" the navy man said agreeably. "Now come on—in you go."

The girl bunched her hair on top of her head and dragged on the tight-fitting rubber helmet. Highlights slid along the surface of the polished latex as she reached up to set the oval mask in place. A moment later she was lowering herself into the tiny rear compartment of the submarine.

Illya climbed into the forward cockpit, turned to give her the thumbs-up sign, and lowered the perspex nacelle over his head and shoulders. The navy man screwed down both the transparent hatches and shortly afterwards they felt the helicopter sinking towards the lake invisible in the darkness below them. The cigar-shaped craft with its twin blisters, despite its aerodynamic shape, lurched sickeningly and swayed from side to side on its guide ropes when the bomb bay doors were opened and the helicopter crew winched them slowly down towards the water. Through the perspex, they could see the drowned valley curving away to the southwest, fifteen or twenty miles of smooth lead foil among the darkness of the jagged hills. Lights pricked the dark to the south and northeast, but they were a long way away. Immediately below, there was not a sign of life.

They hit the water stern first with a ringing slap that

echoed thunderously in the tiny craft. Half a minute later, they were pitching uneasily in the choppy waves agitating the surface of the lake. The helicopter, having activated the automatic release grapples on the guides, rose into the night and clattered away towards Brasilia.

Kuryakin immediately switched on the motors and took the sub beneath the surface. Coralie Simone had a fleeting impression of waves splashing towards her up the inclined surface of the screen that was so close to her eyes, and then they were in a blackness so intense that it almost hurt. She was aware of a complex hum from the electric propulsion system and its auxilaries—and of a dark and heavy chill that pervaded the air in the minute cockpit and numbed her senses.

"We shall have to hurry," Kuryakin's amplified voice split the silence from the intercom by her ear. "The air's very limited and we don't dare use the cylinders in case we have to get out underwater. Can you get the equipment working right away?"

"Of course," the girl said, and she willed her hands to the tasks they had learned that afternoon. There were two systems aboard: the usual echo-sounding device for revealing subterranean topography, other shapes in the sea and so on, and a more modern technique, analogous to the system used in air-to-air missiles, homing on the heat energy released by the motors of the quarry.

"Do you think they'll have the same equipment on their submarine?" she asked as she busied herself with dials and indicators.

"I would guess not," Illya said. "We hope not, anyway. Even if they have it, they'd hardly have it in use. I mean, they'd use the navigational aids, of course—but why would they watch a screen for possible enemy ships when it's their lake and they know they're the only ship in it?"

"I suppose you're right. But if they *did* have it . . . and use it?"

"Then we'd be lost," the agent said shortly. "Are you getting anything interesting yet?"

"It's a bit difficult at first—especially since I'm not really a trained operator. And there are still so many objects on the valley floor—houses, I suppose, and trees and walls and so on—that it's really impossible to sort out . . . Wait a minute! Here's something. . . . It's something big, very big!"

She began reading off figures and Kuryakin concentrated on his dials and controls. "It will be the nuclear submarine, will it, if it proves to be moving?" she asked.

"Bound to be. According to Napoleon, they only test at night—to avoid any possible witnesses, no doubt. What do you see?"

"It *is* moving. —And my goodness, Illya, it must be *enormous!*"

Kuryakin switched on his monitors. "Yes, you're right," he said. "It is pretty generously built. Seems to be on a cross-course some way above us."

"How deep are we?" the girl asked.

"About ten fathoms. From the disturbance, I should judge that the sub's actually on the surface—or at the most only half submerged. We'll go on up and see how near we can get."

Now gaining, now falling behind, the midget submarine stalked the nuclear vessel in the black waters of the lake. The skipper of the Thrush craft was adopting an erratic course, zigzagging from side to side of the reservoir, accelerating and slowing every few minutes.

"He's testing the surface maneuverability," Illya said. "Must be. I only wish we could surface too. It would be so much easier to keep track of him. But we don't dare—there might be a phosphorescent wake, a too-smart lookout, anything. We'll just have to hope he goes in soon."

Once, concentrating too closely on the livid radiance of the radar screens, they almost rammed the tiny craft straight into a massive wall of rock that rose straight from the valley floor. Another time, the nuclear submarine took them by surprise making a tight U-turn and passing almost directly overhead in the opposite direction.

Looking up through their perspex domes at the faint hint of light drifting down from the surface, they watched the great hull—only inches above their eyes, it seemed—

draw smoothly past. A shark shape, sinister and efficient, blotting out the light.

Shortly afterwards, there was a commotion in the water around them and the midget rocked violently. The big submarine was submerging.

"It crash-dived fifty fathoms," Illya exclaimed—it had taken them some time to locate it again on their screens —"and now it's scooting along the floor of the old valley for all it's worth!"

They followed the nuclear craft up to the far end of the dam and then back to the *barrage* again, where they "froze" near the rock face to minimize the risk of detection as the bigger vessel turned. "And off she goes again," Kuryakin said in exasperation. "But the *power* of that thing! Do you realize the speed she's doing on those straight runs? Why, on that last one, she was hitting—"

"Illya!" Coralie's voice was urgent over the intercom. "Be quiet a moment, will you? She's altered course through ninety degrees; she's turned off to port, towards the side of the dam. I think she may be going in."

"Okay. I'll try to catch up and tail her. At the last stage, I'll have to follow her by eye—for the only thing we can do is to follow her into this pen if possible—and hope that nobody spots us before they pump out the water!"

It was a strange journey, the last part of that underwater voyage. Deeper and deeper they plunged, the black water streaming past the two inclined screens, the fragile craft vibrating with the thrust of its screws as the man and the girl bent over their screens concentrating on the luminous blob that represented the quarry they hunted. "We're at forty-three fathoms, Illya," Coralie warned anxiously. "The man said—"

"I can see her!" the Russian exclaimed suddenly. "Look!"

Ahead and below, the faintest hint of luminescence marbled the black. The radiance became discernible, stained the dark depths, wavered and spread, and finally revealed the cigar-shaped nose of their own craft, on which it then cast a discreet highlight. And in front of them, silhouetted against the underwater beam, the huge bulk of the submarine hung like a resting fish.

"Put on your lung and harness"—Illya's voice was low —"and be ready to bale out at any time. No more talking after this."

As she shrugged into the shoulder straps and snapped the clasps about her hips, a series of rectangular planes assembled themselves in the faint illumination into the outline of some building. Monolithic and immense, it jutted from the drowned rock face like a legendary keep seen through a dream, its functional lines distorted and imprecise through the movement of the water. Somewhere near the top a great opening yawned—and it was from this gap in the façade that the light came streaming.

The submarine was moving again, the huge hull sliding quietly into the opening, the green light washing outwards contouring the sophisticated curves of its steel sides.

Kuryakin maneuvered the midget adroitly so that it was placed just behind and to one side of one of the vessel's rear quarters. Together the two ships, like a whale with an enemy pilot fish, sank into the gigantic underwater pen through the opening in the fortress wall. A moment later, colossal double doors rolled across and sealed off the entry. And then slowly, as air was pumped in at the top, the water level began to sink in the chamber.

Ten minutes later the nuclear submarine was resting against a dock on the left-hand side of the pen. The midget was submerged on its offside in the small amount of water that had been left in the chamber. And Illya and Coralie, breathing from the aqualungs on their backs, were just below the surface astern of the Thrush vessel, hoping that nobody would take it into his head to walk to the after rail and look directly down into the water.

Kuryakin raised a cautious head. Grotesquely distorted by the acoustics of the chamber, he heard the sound of feet and voices as the crew trooped ashore and waited their turn to go through the hydraulically controlled double doors leading to the interior of the fortress. There seemed to be no personnel on duty in the pen itself—and indeed why should there be, he thought, since it was really no more than an air-lock between the subterranean fortress and the lake?

When the last footstep had died away, he led the girl on a submerged exploration of the pen. There was about fifteen feet of water left in the chamber and the nuclear submarine was still just afloat. The place must be built, he guessed, directly onto some rocky prominence projecting through the lower parts of the fortress: with such a huge area, it would have been impossible to design a structure robust enough to tolerate all that weight of water if there had been other stories immediately below. Basically, the pen itself was just an enormous box, one end of which was formed by the watertight gates. Ceiling, floor, and wall and one side wall were unbroken by any projection or recess—and the remaining side wall, on the left as you entered through the gates, carried along its whole length the platform against which the vessel was moored. The surface of this quay was a couple of feet above the level of the water slapping and sucking at the submarine's sides. Above it, armored glass slits let in the green light which flooded the chamber.

Before they had quit the pen through the double doors at the far end of the quay, some of the crew had rolled ashore a quantity of steel drums which now lay neatly stacked near the craft's massive stern. Behind the shelter of these, Kuryakin reached up and gripped the edge of the platform to haul himself laboriously from the water. Flopping face down across the wet concrete, gasping, for a moment, he rose gingerly to his feet and held out his hands to Coralie.

They unhitched their aqualungs and propped them up against the drums, turning to survey the great pen now from above water level. The submarine filled exactly half the space available. Everywhere around them, above and on all sides, reminders of how recently the place had been simply an oversize tank obtruded on eye and ear. Moisture streamed down the blank walls, dropped hollowly to the curved decks of the ship from the roof, trickled into the water, and dripped from every ledge and cranny and beam and angle to be seen. The Russian had pulled off his helmet and was halfway out of his frogman suit when Coralie laid a hand on his arm.

"It's going to take an age to get back into these if they're still wet," she whispered. "Don't you think perhaps we should keep them on, just in case we have to leave this way in a hurry?"

Illya shook his head. "What you say is quite true," he said. "But look. . . ." He pointed to the girl's legs.

From her hips down to her ankles, the black rubber suit was beaded with drops of water which slid further down with every muscle she moved. "For ten minutes at least," Kuryakin said, "we'd be leaving wet footprints everywhere. And since our only card to play is surprise, I think we'd better not take the chance."

Coralie nodded, frowning slightly. They stripped off the underwater suits and dropped them in two damply quivering heaps beside the aqualungs. Kuryakin was wearing his favorite jeans with a black turtleneck sweater; the girl, also in black, was in a stretch-nylon cat suit.

"I guess we'd just better leave everything here," Illya said. "They're hidden from all but the closest inspection by these drums—and the midget's out of sight around the stern of this nuclear monster."

From a waterproof satchel attached to his aqualung, the agent produced his Walther, the girl's Berretta, and one or two specialist devices which he stowed in his jeans. Then, moving swiftly but on tiptoe, they strode towards the double doors at the far end of the quay. "This is the part, most of all, where you need to keep your fingers crossed," Illya said. "If there's no way of opening these except by some master switch inside, we're—"

He paused in mid-sentence. As they passed into the embrasure housing the exit from the chamber, the first pair of doors swung open before them with a muffled hiss of compressed air.

"Magic-eye beam," he commented. "They must have an automatic cut-out overriding it once the control to flood the chamber has been actuated—otherwise the lake water would break the beam and the doors would open to let it in and inundate the whole place!"

They walked into the air-lock, waited until the padded doors had swung closed, obeyed the illuminated notice saying in five languages: IMPORTANT! DO NOT ATTEMPT TO OPERATE HANDLE OPENING SECOND PAIR OF DOORS UNTIL RED BULB HAS STOPPED FLASHING!—and then operated the handle.

Beyond the inner doors as they swept apart a short length of empty passage stretched. It terminated in a T-junction with a wall plaque direction indicator.

Kuryakin and the girl flitted soundlessly up. Flattening himself against the wall, the agent listened. On the threshold of hearing, machinery hummed somewhere; louder—although still not very near—a confused murmur of voices surged. In the immediate neighborhood, all seemed silent.

He peered cautiously around the corner.

The two arms of the passage curved symmetrically away from him—as though they were circling some central feature, perhaps a giant shaft—each one boasting a collection of doors on its outer wall which began about forty feet beyond the corner. To the left, the indicators read: BRIEFING . . . OPERATIONS CONTROL . . . COMMUNICATIONS . . . WELFARE . . . LIBRARY. Those pointing to the right were labelled: MAINTENANCE . . . ARMORY . . . CATERING . . . PERSONNEL . . . ELEVATORS TO B, C, ADMINISTRATION AND REACTOR. There was nobody in sight along either arm.

"Right looks more interesting," Illya murmured, "but it's where those voices are coming from—and there's about a hundred and twenty crew members of that sub to account for, besides Heaven knows how many members of their private army. We'll play it safe and take the left!"

With their guns ready, they stole noiselessly into the fortress.

Chapter 12

Hearse Under Water

THE SECOND DOOR on the left of the curving passage stood ajar. Through it, Illya and Coralie Simone could see a fair-sized room equipped with a blackboard and benches rather like a school classroom. In the corner nearest the corridor a large desk littered with papers stood by a green baize board carrying charts and graphs and schedules. The door of the room, which was empty, bore a small plaque on which was engraved the word BRIEFING.

"This must be where the leaders come to get their orders before they set out on their various missions . . ." Kuryakin began. He stopped. Approaching around the curve of the passage, voices distantly echoed.

Seizing the girl's arm, he thrust her through the half-open doorway. "Let's hope whoever it is isn't on his way to a briefing, anyway!" he whispered as he thumbed back the safety catch on his gun. He pushed the door almost shut, and peered through the crack as two officers in khaki and black uniforms passed down the passage and continued on around the bend conversing animatedly in a language Coralie could not place. "Serbo-Croatian," the Russian murmured with a jerk of his head in the direction they had taken. "They were on their way to the canteen. Let's hope the majority of Thrush's personnel are there . . . it's at least the right time for dinner, so maybe we'll be in luck."

Coralie had found among the wall charts behind the desk what appeared to be an exploded diagram of the fortress, showing the relationship of the levels one above the other. "We'll try and memorize it," Illya murmured. "It might save us a lot of time . . . or possibly even our lives."

The basic design of the place could have been represented by three oval pans one above the other, the topmost pan having a short handle—which represented the submarine pen. There seemed, as Illya had surmised, to

137

be a column of rock standing away from the valley wall on which this projection was supported, the remainder of the fortress fitting in between wall and column.

The circular passageway to which the corridor from the pen led was repeated on all three floors of the fortress. On its outer periphery it admitted, on the floor they were on, to a communications complex, to welfare and library sections, to the canteen and to the personnel branch; on the middle floor to living quarters, offices, an armory, the radio room and more catering facilities; and on the lowest level to stores, a cell block and more offices. Within the area circumscribed by the passageway, the bottom floor housed the reactor and the next a circular council chamber which was two stories high and rose to the top floor. From here—on the opposite side of the passage they were traversing—a door appeared to lead to a gallery circling the chamber and some kind of control center at one end of it.

"What I didn't realize," Illya said, "was that they have, of course, this great maintenance unit. Look, we'd have passed it if we had chosen the other branch of the passage. It seems to connect with the pen—I guess there must be sliding doors we didn't notice on the side opposite the quay. After all, even if they didn't actually *make* the sub here and shipped the bits in by air and truck, it had to be *assembled* here and that needs quite an advanced shop."

"Yes," the girl said. "And here's where it came in— look, at one side of the reactor on the lowest floor: it's marked *Truck park*, and there's an arrow pointing to where it says *Double steel doors*. What d'you bet those doors blank off the tunnel leading to the estancia?"

"No takers," the agent grinned. "What I want to find out is how they operate! First of all, though, let's see if we can locate Napoleon. . . . If there's a cell block, he's probably in it."

At the opposite side of the fortress from the corridor leading to the pen, there was apparently a bank of elevators and some stairs. "We'll go down those," he said. "They're probably only used for emergency . . . and this *is* an emergency, anyway!"

Cautiously, they eased open the door and crept out into the passageway. There wasn't a soul in sight. Nor did they see anybody as they sped past the closed doors and gained the open space where the elevators were. Voices were approaching, however, from the direction of the canteen down the other arm of the corridor. Swiftly, the agent pulled the girl after him down the concrete stairway which twisted away around the shaft housing the three elevators.

The rough, curving walls were glistening with moisture, though the air current surging up from the depths at the command of some extractor plant behind them was dry and arid. Increasingly, the two of them were aware of the relentless cold pressure of those countless tons of water leaning, day in and day out, on the roof of the fortress. And as though to underline the point, the string of low power naked bulbs set in the slanting ceiling of the stairway dimmed abruptly and then slowly flared again—though not quite to their former brightness, the girl thought with a shiver. Still, it was probably just some fluctuation in the output of the reactor below them. . . . The sound of voices above swelled; the echoes expanded, then dwindled as the people talking passed the entrance to the shaft and continued on around the passageway.

They crept into the reflected light from the landing on B Level. Footsteps and voices echoed here too, advancing and receding in some numbers. Elevator doors opened and shut and they heard the cages whining away upwards beyond the wall of their stairway. It was some minutes before Kuryakin was satisfied that it was safe to peer around the last corner and prospect the landing. He drew back suddenly. A solitary man was waiting for an elevator to return.

Two minutes later, after the doors had hissed shut and the lift had ascended again, he ventured to peer once more. The landing was empty.

Beckoning to the girl to follow him, he raced across and plunged down the further flight of stairs towards the bottom level. Here it was quieter, the lights were even dimmer, and there was no sign of any of the fortress's inhabitants.

There was no sign, either, of Napoleon Solo. There were six featureless cells in the cul-de-sac leading off the circular passage. And all of them were empty.

"What now?" Coralie asked, seeing the momentary flicker of despair on Illya's face. "Is there anywhere else we can look for your friend?"

He shook his head slowly, his eyes somber. "Anywhere," he said. "He could be anywhere . . . alive or dead. We shall simply have to proceed with the action as though—"

"But I thought your friend—"

"The mission," Illya said almost savagely. "The mission comes first. I told you what Waverly said. We'll try to get back to the control room on the top floor and see what we can do there."

They completed the circuit of the corridor, past a half-open door hedged with red notices warning unauthorized personnel without protective clothing to keep out—and through which they glimpsed behind coils of tubing a segment of the great reactor's silver sphere. As they approached the elevators again, they saw a number of trucks drawn up in two ranks facing an immense pair of doors on rails. To Kuryakin's astonishment, there seemed to be no guard, no sentry box, only a series of metal housings flanking the doors with inset magic eye discs and an old-fashioned set of stop-go lights.

"The whole thing's electronically controlled," he said softly. "If we only could get to that control room . . . Come on!"

They skirted the empty trucks and gained the staircase. By the time they reached the A Level again, they were both panting. But they were in luck: they had seen nobody. "Come on," the Russian urged again. "The door's a little way further around the curve, on the inside wall. I saw it in the distance when we left the briefing room."

Suddenly—bullets splatted against the concave surface of the outer wall. Simultaneously, from behind them, the sharp crack of an automatic, three times, reverberated in the narrow corridor.

"Run!" Illya yelled, hauling her after him, pelting further, further, further around the curve of the convex inner wall. The uniformed officer he had seen out of the corner of his eye as he glanced over his shoulder fired again and again, trying to hit them with ricochets off the outer wall now that they were invisible to him.

As they ran, voices shouted. Footsteps started after them from somewhere out of sight. A door in the outer wall opened and two women in D.A.M.E.S. uniform emerged just in front of them. One was carrying a black frogman suit over her arm.

"Apologies, madam," Kuryakin said hurriedly as he snatched the heavy rubber garment from her hands, twisted it around her head and pushed her, reeling, across to the other side of the passage. The second woman swore violently and began to tug something from the pocket of her uniform jacket. Without breaking her stride, Coralie Simone slashed a backhanded blow across and caught her Karate-style on the side of the neck. She dropped straight to the floor, rolled against the calves of the woman struggling to free herself from the folds of the diving suit, and brought her down too.

Kuryakin and the girl sprinted on. The shooting from behind had stopped when the marksman had come into sight of the two D.A.M.E.S. But now there were heavy footsteps pounding *towards* them from around the curve ahead. A deeper report thundered in the confined space and a slug chiseled a groove in the wall beside Coralie's head.

"I was afraid of that," the agent panted. "Sent . . . friend . . . around the other way . . . cut us off." He dropped to one knee. Along the surface of the outer wall where it curved out of sight ahead of them, a grotesquely distorted shadow was approaching. He sighted along the barrel of the PPK and fired.

There was a puff of plaster dust where the bullet gouged itself a channel. Before the screech of the ricochet had died away, both footsteps and shadow had halted. Behind, too, there was silence now.

"Let's go," Illya whispered, his lips close to Coralie's ear, "before they realize they can sidle up to us along

141

the inner wall. If the control room door's near enough, we'll reach it before we come in sight of the man ahead of us."

"Suppose it's locked?" the girl murmured as they began to move.

Illya merely shrugged. There were more footsteps in the distance now, and a susurrus of low voices asking questions somewhere in the circle of corridor behind them.

Backs to the inner wall, they inched towards the elusive door. Slowly, inexorably, the corridor uncoiled before their advance . . . and as relentlessly, the inner wall remained exasperatingly blank.

With a lightning-like pounce, Kuryakin leaped suddenly to the far side and ripped off a shot, left, right, in each direction. There was a distant scrambling of feet as he jumped back again, a single shot from their left, the bigger caliber gun with the deeper tone, and then a cry of protest from the other side as the slug screamed to the right.

"They're too close up to shoot at us now, really," Illya said. "Every shot's in danger of bouncing on and hitting their own people around the curve. . . . The door's not far now: I could see it from the other side."

And sure enough, the heavy, flush-fitting steel door, like the entrance to a warship's cabin, was soon sliding around the curve towards them. Once it was fully in view, the Russian sprang forwards and grasped the handle. It turned easily in his grip and the door swung inwards. With a gasp of relief, he motioned the girl through, closed the door, and dropped two steel struts in place across it. They were in.

The door admitted directly to a narrow gallery which ran all the way around the walls of a huge circular room on the floor below. Halfway around to the left, a staircase spiraled to the lower floor; and opposite this to the right the gallery bore a glassed-in projection resembling the control room of a television or recording studio. Through the huge panes, they could see colored lights winking, the gleam of stainless steel levers, banks of bright terminals. There were a number of desks with telephones on them distributed about the floor space below, but the majority of the enormous room was occupied by a circular table so vast that the seven people grouped along one sector of it were dwarfed by its size.

A woman in the now familiar green uniform was standing talking to the thin man with the skull-like face at the center of the group as they came through the door.

". . . took the prisoners through and left them on the quay as you ordered," she was saying. "The girl was a little difficult and I had to subdue her, but the man was still quiet. Mr. Greerson's shoes do their job well."

A bony man lost in a voluminous brown suit smiled thinly. "After that," the woman continued, "I locked the double—" She stopped, staring up at the gallery.

Every member of the group reacted differently to the sight of Kuryakin and Coralie Simone and the sound of hammering which had broken out on the steel door behind them. The Negro, Hernando, gaped in astonishment without moving. Two thick-set, heavy men pushed their chairs back from the table and sat tensely watchful. The woman's hard face creased into an expression of contempt. A heavy, gray man cowered and seemed to shrink into his chair. And the man called Greerson sprang backwards, tipping over his seat as a gun blossomed in his right hand spitting fire. Quick as he was, though, the leader with the skeletal face was more rapid still. Only his hand moved, diving into the space between his lapels while the rest of him remained motionless as a statue. But the gun with which it reappeared had fired twice while Greerson was still in mid-air.

Illya and the girl had ducked down behind the solid steel balustrade of the gallery and were moving towards the control room as fast as they could. The first of the leader's shots passed so close to the agent's head that he felt the scorching breath of its passage on his neck.

"Greerson! Quick!" they heard the man shouting below. "The spiral staircase! Enfilade them before they reach the control room! You, Schwarz, run underneath . . . you know, Plan D!"

Feet pounded amid the hubbub of voices, and then the leader called again: "Moraes—stay where you are, man. Or get under the table if you're so scared." The tone was full of contempt. "You up there—Mestoso!—we're relying on you. . . ."

Mestoso? Greerson's feet were stamping up the staircase on the far side of the gallery. Who was Mestoso? Where— Just in time, Kuryakin caught the flicker of movement behind the windows of the control room. It was a difficult shot, across the curve of the gallery and through a sheet of glass angled away and obscured by reflections, but it had to be quick. The Walther roared in the confined space between wall and balustrade.

The man Mestoso, standing on a table with a submachine gun ready to rake them from above, leaned forward out of the reflections and touched the glass. At the same time the entire pane seemed to leap outwards, to hang frozen in the air for a moment, and then to plunge floorwards in gigantic shards. After it, lazily somersaulting, arced the body of the man with the gun. In the appalling crash of the plate glass on the floor below, Illya and Coralie gained the door of the control room and slipped inside.

"Check what's happening down below," the agent panted. "I've got to find . . . have to cut off all the troops and submarine crew in the canteen somehow . . . must be something like watertight bulkheads . . ."

While he scanned the banks of dials and screens, the girl peered over and into the room below.

The big gray man, Moraes, seemed to have been cut by a fragment of flying glass. He was sitting on the floor, looking owlishly at the blood streaming from a gash in the sleeve of his jacket. The rest of them had retired out of sight beneath the gallery—though they couldn't have left the room, for the only lower-level exit door was in full view on the far side of the room. Of Greerson there was no sign: he must have gained the top of the spiral stairs and must now be worming his way towards them around one or the other side of the gallery. . . .

Illya was intent about a great slanting control board at the back of the room. It was covered in levers moving in labeled slots and there was a console full of knobs in front of it and a series of three illuminated screens behind.

"Look!" he exclaimed excitedly. "These screens are schematic diagrams of the three floors of the fortress. And the place *is* divided into watertight compartments; there *are* bulkheads partitioning it in case of flooding. So here's our chance of blocking off half the opposing forces—if we're lucky and get them on the far side of the watertight doors! Anyway, here goes. . . ."

He spun a small wheel on the console until an arrow on its perimeter pointed to the words MAXIMUM POWER. Then, staring fixedly at the screens, he began hauling the levers set in the board. As each one moved, a bar of red light blocked off some portion of the diagram above.

"A-7 and A-9," he muttered, his eyes roving the screens until they located the references. "That'll be the two top-floor doors to the canteen. There . . . that should have them sealed off. We have already done the ones below. Now let's see. . . . B-12 and 14—*there!*—should barricade the living quarters below; and *this*—B-13, is it?—"Yes, B-13 will keep anyone from getting at the armory—"

Glass splintered to his left. A needle spun emptily around a black dial pierced with a small hole as the pieces tinkled to the floor. The girl was firing her Beretta at a section of balustrade a third of the way around the gallery.

"Greerson," she said succinctly. "Obviously he's not risking a straight attack from either side to enfilade us. He'll just keep popping up here and there from across the well, because he knows one of us has to concentrate on the controls and the other can't watch the whole—*Look out!*"

Kuryakin flung himself to the floor as she loosed off two shots, at the other side of the gallery now. But the gunman had already dropped behind the shelter of the steel balustrade. A torn sheet of paper fluttered down from a clip projecting from the wall just behind where the Russian had been standing. He pulled the girl down beside him. "Thanks," he said soberly. "That was just in time." He drew up the hem of his sweater. Around his waist, a lightweight, pocketed band something like a cartridge belt was fastened. From one of the compartments he withdrew a small, square object with a sliding switch on one side.

"Okay," he said. "Draw his fire. I'll pretend to be busy at the control board again. You sweep the right hand arc of the gallery. If I know the psychology of these boys, this will be the time he'll shoot for the second time from exactly the same place."

The girl turned deliberately away from the section of gallery where the last shot had been fired and stared to her right. Kuryakin had his back to the main room. He was bending over the console—but one hand shielded a black-dialed pressure gauge in such a way that it acted as a mirror. A few seconds later, he saw the reflected head of Greerson rise cautiously above the balustrade exactly where he had said it would. The agent whirled. Instantly, the head dropped from sight. But it wasn't a gunshot target Kuryakin wanted: it was enough to know the section of gallery Greerson was in. He sprang to the glassless control room window.

His right arm straightened like a baseball pitcher's. The small, square object sailed across the well and dropped down between the balustrade and the wall.

There was a subdued, flat detonation and a surge of smoke. Something rose above the level of the rail for an instant, threshing, and then dropped from sight. There were no more shots from across the gallery.

"Small grenades are very useful in confined spaces," Illya said, "even if they are only made with bakelite covers. Now, let's see—the watertight bulkheads are closed, all those that can be of any use to us. That leaves us free in the central area with the six people below and any other military who happened to be in the passageways when I started to close the doors."

"And the reactor?"

The agent gestured towards the indicator board. On the section detailing the lowest floor, the central rondel was bracketed at all its entrances by illuminated red lines. "It's the only part of the middle bit protected," he said. "Now we have to go to this other board and—ah—

pull a few strings to *open* things . . . the doors to the tunnel, for example."

"But, Illya, what are we going to do? I mean, there are only two of us, after all . . . and at least one has to stay here in case they come back and reopen all the doors you've closed. And if that one was me, I wouldn't like to guarantee that I could hold out against all of them. On the other hand, what could I do out there if *you* stayed?"

"The point is well taken," Kuryakin said. "You couldn't complete the mission if I stayed here; I wouldn't be allowed to if you did. Ergo, we send for help . . . and don't forget, they wouldn't come *back* here: they are here. There are still six of them underneath."

"What do you mean, call for help?" the girl said.

Illya produced the tiny transceiver from his belt. "Waverly," he said. "He's waiting with O'Rourke and others not far from the estancia. If I can find some way of operating the *far* end of the tunnel, they can come right in. If not, they'll have to blast their way through. In either case, as you point out, we won't be able to get to the maintenance section and put the missiles out of action without them."

"And the second part of the mission—your friend?"

As Kuryakin frowned, the downstairs door to the council chamber was flung violently open. The crash of the steel door against the wall was drowned in the clamor of the sub-machine guns held by the two uniformed men standing there.

Once more they dropped to the floor—noticing from the corners of their eyes a blur of movement from beneath the gallery towards the soldiers and their covering fire.

The agent crawled a little way along the gallery as the staccato tattoo of slugs ripped into the walls and ceiling above them. After a moment he ducked up, gun in hand, and fired a single shot. The clatter of the Thompsons ceased. Something fell metallically to the floor. A moment later the door slammed again.

Kuryakin rose to his feet. "Got one of them," he said, blowing the curl of smoke from the gun's barrel. "It was just a diversion to get the top brass away. But we'll let 'em go: it's easier for us without them down there."

He turned his back on the chamber below and began studying the masses of equipment stacked around the control room.

"Look here," he said, opening the lid of what looked like an oversized record-player cabinet. "There's the usual ground-glass screen in the lid—complete with schematic diagrams and pilot lights in a pattern I don't recognize—plus levers and knobs on top of the chassis in the box itself. And the only identification is this strip here saying 'Section E.' Now if E could stand for *estancia* . . ."

He never knew what extra sense made him turn his head at that moment. A faint current of air, perhaps; something moving reflected in a bright surface in the corner of his eye; a sound too small to be registered by the conscious mind. . . . Whatever it was, he did turn—and saw the bludgeon on its way down to the back of his skull.

As his breath hissed in with astonishment, he lurched to one side with an arm automatically raised to ward off the blow.

The girl, pivoting too, gave a gasp of alarm as she took in the scene in a single agonized glance: the yawning trapdoor which had been silently opened behind a bank of teleprinters, the attacker—he was one of the two thick-set men who had been at the table when they'd come in—with murderous expression and upraised arm, the whistle of the blackjack. . . .

It was too late for Kuryakin to escape the blow completely. The blackjack glanced off his wrist and thudded into the muscle between his collar bone and the point of his shoulder, forcing a shout of pain from his lips and paralyzing his arm.

As the Walther crashed to the floor from his numbed hand, the man swung around in a smooth spiral of controlled energy, knocked the Beretta from the girl's grasp with the truncheon and—before the little gun had gone spinning out of the shattered window to crash to the floor below—had swung back on the rebound and knocked her sprawling to the far side of the room.

148

Illya reeled, pain searing his whole side. Desperately, through blinded eyes, he fixed his gaze on the blackjack and groped upwards to fasten wiry fingers on the wrist that wielded it.

The big man snarled, shaking the slight figure of the agent from side to side as a mongoose shakes a snake. But eventually the crushing judo grip forced apart his fingers and the blackjack clattered down. Swearing, he collapsed suddenly to the ground, dragging Illya on top of him. The Russian brought up his knee to the man's solar plexus and forced his sound forearm under the blue chin. But the attacker knew all the tricks in the wrestling trade—and he was formidably strong, too. At a distance, Kuryakin could have held his own, but they were already too much at close quarters for him to stand a chance.

The thug rolled over, holding the agent to him in a bear hug, caromed off the teleprinters, and sat up with Illya in a scissors grip. Three times, viciously, his fist jarred the Russian's head—and then again they were locked together toe to toe, wrist to wrist, with every muscle shrieking to sound out a weakness in the opponent's guard.

Abruptly, Kuryakin abandoned the trial of strength and went limp. For a moment he was bent over the opening left by the trapdoor—then, wrapping his legs around the man's hips, he dropped through, dragging the thug with him.

From below came the sound of splintering wood and a strangled shout.

The girl had picked herself up, sobbing, some time before. The Walther had been kicked somewhere under a cabinet in the fight and she had been circling the struggling men, not knowing how to help. Her mascara had run and her nose was bleeding. Now, with a cry of alarm, she sprang to the edge and looked down.

Amid the remnants of a table, the Thrush man had Kuryakin bent backwards like a bow in the agonizing grip known as the Boston Crab. In wrestling bouts this dangerous hold almost always results in a submission; if there is no referee and the pressure is continued, a spine snaps.

Aghast, Coralie watched the veins on the big man's temple and arms bulge as Kuryakin's eyes turned up and his face broke out in sweat.

"*Illya!*" she screamed.

"Pen . . . pen . . ." the agent choked. "Quick . . . floor."

In anguish, her eyes swept the boards below. In the exertion of the struggle, most of the contents of Illya's belt had been spilled out onto the ground. Among them was a slim cylinder resembling a ballpoint.

Without hesitating, she dropped through the trapdoor like a stone, hit the floor with a numbing impact, staggered, recovered herself—and reached for the tiny device. There was a button at one end.

Almost in a reflex action, before he had realized what was happening, she had pointed the other end at the thug's face and thumbed the button. There was a shrill hiss of gas escaping under pressure. The man's eyes widened, his mouth split open in an almost ludicrous expression of surprise, and he pitched forward as the agent collapsed with a groan of relief.

Ten minutes later, when the girl had tidied herself up and Kuryakin had recovered sufficiently to climb the ladder back to the control room, they began again to speculate whether the cabinet with the screen in the lid was a control for the outer gates of the tunnel.

"We can only try," Illya said. He stretched out his hand and grasped one of the levers on the control panel. "Let's see what E.1 will do . . ."

"*I wouldn't, Mr. Kuryakin. I really wouldn't.*" The voice came from behind them.

Together, they whirled. Zig-zag lines chased themselves across the screen of a small monitor television set just above the shattered window. Above it was a fixed, closed-circuit camera. The voice had undoubtedly come from here.

"*It may not do what the label says, you see,*" the voice went on. "*Because although you have unfortunately incapacitated the man we left behind us, he had done his work first.*"

"I have no idea what you mean," Illya said, looking directly at the camera. Below it, white patches streamed across the screen, to coalesce and finally assemble with the darker zig-zags into a picture of three men and a woman sitting behind a control panel similar to the one behind him. The woman was the one who had been in the chamber; the men were Moraes, Hernando, and the man with the skull-like face. It was the latter who was speaking.

"*I will tell you,*" he drawled. "*Ah—I see from your face that you can now see us. We have been able to see you all the time. . . . When you burst in and interrupted our meeting, you may or may not have heard the lady here report that she had delivered two prisoners somewhere, a man and a woman.*"

"Well?"

"*The place she had taken them to was the submarine pen.*"

"I'm afraid I don't see—"

"*Where she had left them and double-locked the exit doors. There is now no conceivable way in which they can reënter the fortress.*"

"So?"

"*The man is your colleague, Mr. Napoleon Solo; the woman is a foolish girl who for some reason tried to help him.*"

Illya caught his breath. "Even so," he said, "I don't quite—"

"*We now come back to Schwarz, the man we left behind,*" the leader with the skeletal face said smoothly. "*You may have heard me instruct him, at one point in the proceedings, to put Plan D into operation?*"

"Okay, I'll bite," Kuryakin said, the hairs prickling on the nape of his neck. "What *is* Plan D?"

"*An emergency plan evolved in case anyone should temporarily take over the control room. It is very simple: Schwarz merely disconnected some of the leads from the controls—and then replaced them in a different order.*"

"And that means?" Illya asked with a dry mouth.

"That when you pull lever A or twist Knob E, you may not now observe reaction A or reaction B on the indicator screens. Not necessarily. You may operate lever A and set in train reaction X."

The agent stared at the screen, his mind racing.

"You might find—to give a more concrete example—that you twisted a knob to open the gates to a tunnel . . . and succeeded only in flooding a submarine pen. Which would be awkward for your friend Solo.

There was a long silence.

Kuryakin turned and walked to the trapdoor, looking down into the room below. All along the back wall, metal housings like giant fuse boxes hung open—and inside, festooned like the fronds of anemone and weed in some fantastic undersea pool, he could see hundreds upon hundreds of strands of wire in dozens of different colors.

". . . And not one of those leads is labeled," the voice went on. *"Nor are the leads above and below the connection boxes necessarily the same color or combination of colors."*

It was quite true. From where he stood, Illya could see. He deliberately turned his back on the TV monitor and surveyed the control board. Any of the wheels or levers whose function, according to the coded numerals and letters on them and repeated on the indicator above, was to open or shut doors, operate fire extinguishers, raise or lower screens or put magic eye circuits out of operation . . . any of these might in actuality open sluices which could bring thousands of tons of water in upon the defenseless Solo and his companion in their subterranean prison.

"You've been lucky so far," the voice said persuasively. *"You have managed to seal off a good proportion of our forces because the watertight bulkhead doors are excluded from Plan D—for obvious reasons of security. But will you be so lucky next time?"*

"Look, I don't know who you are," Illya began, still with his back to the camera.

"The name is Wassermann. A member of the Council of Thrush, along with Senhor Moraes and Hernando

here. We are but three of many. You cannot possibly succeed against us. Why do you not simply give up? The odds are too heavily stacked against you."

For answer, Kuryakin reached out and grasped a lever.

"Illya!" the girl cried. "You can't! Surely—"

"Be quiet!" the agent rasped. "Remember what Waverly said."

"Never mind Waverly. You can't take the risk."

"I said be quiet."

"You are foolish, my boy." It was Hernando speaking now. His lined face was in close up on the monitor screen. *"We are in a small extra control room here, next to the radio room. We cannot overrule any actions you take—but they are duplicated on our indicators. Think. You may bring death to your friends with that little lever; you may cut off the oxygen supply to the whole fortress; you may douse the room you are in with foam; you may over-fuel the reactor . . ."*

Kuryakin set his teeth and pulled firmly on the lever.

"Watch the big board in the corner," Wassermann said. *"The pen is an oblong at the moment glowing in green. The reactor is a red circle below it. If it is over-fueled, the red glow becomes intermittent. When water is admitted to the pen, it goes blank, then slowly fills with blue."*

The agent's eyes were sternly fixed on the small indicator in the lid of the cabinet before him. He was staring at the red bar marking what he thought was the closed exit to the tunnel—waiting for it to go green.

A sharp cry from the girl dragged his eyes to the other board.

The rectangle symbolizing the submarine pen was no longer green. As he watched, horrorstruck, a luminous blue line appeared at the bottom of the oblong, slowly thickening upwards.

With a smothered exclamation, he seized the lever and struggled to push it back up again. There was a chuckle from the television screen. *"Oh, no, Mr. Kuryakin"*—it was Moraes speaking this time—*"you cannot do that! The action is irreversible. Think it out. There must be a censor overriding all controls while the place is filling: we could not have water levels rising and falling like yo-yos with expensive machinery like nuclear submarines in there, now could we? The 'Exhaust Pen' control will remain inoperative until thirty minutes after the chamber is full. To make sure nobody can empty it while the craft is maneuvering, you know. By which time, of course, your friend . . ."* He shrugged eloquently.

There was a click and the sound went off. The vision dwindled to a tiny white square, brightened for an instant, and then vanished.

Illya dashed to the trapdoor, jumped to the floor below, and began frenziedly searching among the gaily colored leads. But Wassermann had been right: the task was hopeless. There were hundreds. It would have taken an expert electrician hours to trace them all back and check the altered connections through the fused junction boxes. Dispiritedly, he turned and hauled himself back up the ladder. The girl had set her back to him—and the oblong on the indicator board was blue more than three-quarters of the way up.

Twelve minutes later, as the Russian played desultorily with the levers on the cabinet devoted to Section E, the rectangle glowed blue all over.

Shortly after that, the TV screen suddenly came to life again. The picture was grainy and blurred, but the sound was fine. Wassermann appeared to be in some small room busy with pipes and dials. *"Just to thank you, Mr. Kuryakin, for filling the chamber and allowing us to make our escape in the submarine,"* he said suavely. *"You have blocked off five missiles in the maintenance unit—but there is one aboard the ship. I am speaking from the conning tower, and we are on our way to the far end of the lake to prepare for firing. . . . Buenos Aires, I think. . . . It's not the full-scale effect we planned, but it'll be better than nothing. And just in case your friends outside should be stronger than we are, it's just as well, rather than risk failure, to get the Thrush mission at least partly—"*

The screen blacked out, losing both sound and vision

in mid-sentence. Fragments of glass lying shattered on the floor jingled as the control room trembled beneath their feet. The lights dimmed and then brightened as a long rumbling roar, felt rather than actually heard, shivered and reverberated around the fortress.

"Illya!" the girl was saying despite herself. "Look!" She pointed at the ground-glass screen in the lid of the Section E cabinet.

Some of the controls he had idly operated had worked: for across the entrance to the diagram tunnel what had formerly been a red bar now showed bright green.

Kuryakin slumped into a chair. He pulled out his transceiver and held it to his mouth.

"Hello, Mr. Waverly," he said wearily, thumbing the button. "You may find one or two sentries outside, but as far as the tunnel's concerned, you can come in right now. . . ."

Chapter 13

Illya Changes His Mind

"THAT WAS thoughtful of you to leave those aqualungs and diving suits behind the drums," Napoleon Solo said. "Without them we'd both have been in Davy Jones' locker for keeps! But when I heard the water come bubbling in from the vent beneath the submarine, we climbed onto the drums and saw those things down below."

"I can't understand why nobody saw you when they came in in their own diving gear to board the sub," Illya said.

"That was the drums again! They didn't float, you see: they had been used as ballast to simulate the missile payload—and, being filled with concrete, they just sat on the quay and we sat behind them."

"And you saw our midget submarine . . . ?"

155

"As soon as the Thrush craft pulled out, there she was waiting for us on the other side. I guessed she would have the usual small, single HE torpedo underslung, so we hopped aboard and set sail after the target bird. Then it was simply a matter of waiting until she was far enough away not to damage the fortress when she went up."

"But the nuclear missile itself didn't actually explode?" Coralie Simone asked.

"Oh, no. It takes a small atom bomb to trigger off a thermonuclear device; ordinary high explosive isn't hot enough to start the reaction. But we made quite a big bang with our little tin-fish because she was carrying quite a lot of conventional armament and I was lucky enough to hit it. . . ."

They were sitting in the Departure Lounge at Brasilia airport, waiting for the flight to be called which was to take Solo, Waverly and Alice Lerina back to Rio and thence to New York. To one side, the vast bulk of Manuel O'Rourke reared from his wheelchair, with the boy, Rafael, in attendance. Since the Irishman had sent his Cadillac careening through the tunnel at the head of a column of state troopers, scattering two separate nests of machine-gunners and personally helping the authorities to round up the troops within the fortress from that chair, the young car-dispenser, with the light of hero-worship in his eyes, had never left his side.

"One thing I can't understand at all," Illya said. He turned to Waverly, who was stuffing half an ounce of tobacco into the bowl of an enormous briar. "I got a message at San Felipe telling me to go to a certain rendezvous—and there I met O'Rourke, who put me in radio touch with you."

"Yes, Mr. Kuryakin," Waverly said. "Well?"

"Well, how did that come about?"

"I thought Mr. O'Rourke explained. He could get there quicker by car than if he had waited for me to arrive from New York and we had come on together by plane. That way, he could contact you in advance and talk to me by radio as soon as—"

"Yes, yes, yes," Kuryakin said with what was for him a near-miss at exasperation. "What I mean is—one, how did you know O'Rourke *could* contact me; two, how did you know he'd be equipped with all that special radio stuff; and three, how did you know about him at all? How did you know to contact *him?* How did you know he could be trusted? I'd never mentioned him in my reports on this affair."

Waverly coughed. "Both you and Mr. Solo mentioned him in your reports after the—ah—I believe we code-named it the Radioactive Camel Affair," he said. "I considered that a man with his capacity for gathering information should be persuaded to put that facility to work for the common good."

"But we thought he had been killed in Casablanca! I didn't know he was still alive until I saw him by chance in Rio."

"Our people made certain inquiries," Waverly said vaguely.

"Do you mean to say," Solo put in, amazed, "that Mr. O'Rourke is one of us? D'you mean he's on the payroll and we didn't know?"

"Doesn't always do to let the right hand know what the left hand is doing," the head of U.N.C.L.E.'s Policy and Operations Section said gruffly, stowing his unlit pipe in one pocket and searching in the other for matches.

"Ah . . . yes, sir," Solo said diplomatically, exchanging a wry glance with Illya.

"Sure it sometimes gets an idea into a fella's skull more easily if you let him discover it himself," O'Rourke said with an easy smile. "Isn't that so, Rafael?"

"It does so," the boy said. "And it's a queer ould life we'd be having if there was no place left for the adventurers at-all."

Waverly had lit a match and appeared to be surprised that there was no pipe in his mouth for it to ignite. A trim stewardess in a dark blue uniform passed them as an incomprehensible gargle of Portuguese poured from the PA speakers. "It is forbidden to smoke," she said severely, "while proceeding to the aircraft. That is your flight being called."

Napoleon Solo rose to his feet. His face was still swollen and bruised from the beating he had taken from Greerson, but there was the old light in his eye as he placed one palm under Alice Lerina's elbow and guided her toward the door. "Okay," he said. "We're on our way. In view of various favors past received, Mrs. Lerina and I have a date with a parole officer somewhere on the West Coast, so that her life can be put in order again. After that, I hope we may have a date with each other."

"It depends," the girl said, "on the way you behave during that long plane journey!"

Waverly was already halfway to the aircraft, deep in conversation with O'Rourke and Rafael.

Coralie Simone and Illya watched them go with indulgent smiles. There was a genuine detachment of D.A.M.E.S. on their way to help with the local population while the Brazilian authorities decided what was to be done with the dam and the empty power house attached to it. Coralie was to wait and take charge of the women when they arrived—and the Russian had decided to spend the week's leave due to him in her company.

The girl took his arm. "Illya dear," she said, "do you think we'll have time to make a quick trip to Bahia before the girls' plane arrives tomorrow night? There's two churches and a sixteenth century presbytery I'd love to take you to there."

The agent was looking at her aghast.

"Churches?" he said faintly. "Presbytery?"

"Why, yes," Coralie Simone said, tucking his hand under her arm and walking firmly away from the bar. "You must remember, after all, that we are the Daughters of America *Missionary* Emergency Service. . . ."

But Illya Kuryakin had already pulled free and burst through the swing doors onto the field.

The plane, a glisten of stressed metal at the far end of the runway, was turning into the wind. "Napoleon!" he shouted, sprinting across the hot tarmac towards it.

158

"Napoleon! Wait for me, Napoleon! . . . I've changed my mind. Stop the plane—I want to come with you! . . . Napoleon . . ."

If you have missed any full-length U.N.C.L.E. adventures starring Napoleon Solo and Illya Kuryakin, ask your newsdealer for them, or use order form below: